Elder Mountain

A Journal of Ozarks Studies

Issue 11

Missouri State University-West Plains

ISSN 1946-0511

Elder Mountain: A Journal of Ozarks Studies is published
once a year by the Department of English at Missouri State
University-West Plains.

Major funding for Issue Eleven of *Elder Mountain* was
provided by Lynn Morrow.

Submission Guidelines

A juried journal, *Elder Mountain* seeks Ozarks-focused manuscripts from all disciplinary perspectives (particularly anthropology, economics, folklore, geography, geology, history, literature, music, and political science) as well as interdisciplinary approaches. In addition, high-quality, Ozarks-oriented short stories, poems, and works of creative nonfiction are of keen interest, as is visual art that examines the Ozarks.

Only electronic submissions are accepted and may be sent as a Word attachment to PhillipHowerton@MissouriState.edu. Deadline for first consideration is April 1.

Well-crafted, thesis-driven articles free of discipline-specific jargon have the greatest likelihood of acceptance. Articles should use the documentation style appropriate to the discipline.

Carefully wrought short stories and essays free of common Ozark stereotypes will receive appreciative consideration. Creative prose pieces should be a maximum of 5000 words.

Poems may range in style from formal to free verse. Strong imagery and intelligently rendered content are attractive qualities.

For visual art we seek images (photography, paintings, ink drawings, etc.) suitable for reproduction in black and white. We prefer that images be sent electronically as a JPG, PNG, or TIF file. Include a one- or two-page artist's statement.

Simultaneously submitted or previously published work will not be considered.

Elder Mountain reserves first North American serial rights only. All other rights revert to the authors and artists upon publication in *Elder Mountain*.

Table of Contents

Fiction

Nonfiction

Photography

Reviews

Editor's Note

Welcome to Issue 11 of *Elder Mountain: A Journal of Ozark Studies*! Everything changes, and the Ozarks is a changing place. Although some changes are welcome, they are often accompanied by a sense of loss. In fact, a sense of place and an attachment to a region are almost always linked with a sense of loss, and a connection between change and loss run through this issue of *Elder Mountain*.

Regional change is evident in much of this work as the contributors consider the past, present, and future of this region. Reflecting on the past, Wilson Allen and Jim Hamilton consider some of what the region might have lost in so-called progress. In the present, John Mort and Michelle Collins Anderson examine change in relationships between people. And looking to the future, Cathie English examines the possibilities of creating, examining, and sustaining a sense of place.

Some authors focus their work on change but use the feeling of loss to move the reader back in time. Others touch on losses with some humor and remark that some things needed to be lost, and still others give their work a subtle feeling of loss that grows almost imperceptibly until the final word is reached. Jenny Crews, Jim Hamilton, and Marcus Cafagña all engage some level and sense of loss.

This issue presents sixteen poems, three short stories, nine essays, and ten book reviews —the work of twenty writers. I would like to thank all these contributors and the readers for their interest in Ozark studies and for supporting *Elder Mountain*. I also wish to thank Dr. Howerton for inviting me to serve as editor. I have enjoyed learning about the Ozarks and connecting with the amazing people involved in Ozarks studies.

Faith Collins

Peele's Barn

Wilson Allen

Old Man Peele was a master carpenter,
and he laid the entire barn out in the grass
before neighbors arrived to raise it.
No nails were needed in the frame,
which he had sawn from white oaks,
for every joint and juncture, every mortise
and tenon met and matched as he had foreseen.
He had known all that would need to be
done and when and in what order. It was raised
in two days, six were not needed, and it
was built so well that it outlived the old man
and his family, and outlived the mode of life
and farm that produced it. Now only a poet
or folklorist is found foolish enough to trust
its loft ladder and loft floor and to peer
through cracks at the lost world outside.

Black Cemetery Outside of Town

Wilson Allen

The county cemetery census[1] grants
the place no name, listing it as "Negro Graves,"
and states it is *about* one-half mile south
of town and then a *short* quarter mile west
of the road in the corner of woods
near an open field, that it contains *maybe*
eight to ten fieldstone markers overgrown
with underbrush which *legend* says belong
to a black man *called* Art and his family,
that Art was murdered *or* died when his house
burned, and that the graves are *possibly* from
the late 1800s. All the details are uncertain.
Distance from town is uncertain, location
is uncertain, birth dates are unknown,
causes and dates of death are unknown,
names are unknown, the number of graves
is uncertain, their lives are unknown.
For this family, only death was certain.

[1] *Webster County, Missouri: Cemetery Inscriptions*, 1980, pp. 62.

Dirty Old Man

John Mort

It was late March and warm. Jim watched the road.

Sixty years before, give or take, he walked down that road to school. It was paved now, or rather pot-holed; the county would be wise to scrape off the asphalt and run a grader like they used to. Maybe the road wasn't worth maintaining. It came to a dead end in less than a mile because of the Interstate, curving like a scythe blade through what had been the farm's only fertile field.

The mail went around three, though there was nothing in it anymore. Jim remembered an Australian pen-pal from age ten—he thought of her as Adelaide, but that was the name of her city. He wondered what had happened to Adelaide.

He always waved to the mail carriers, and many days they were the only humans he saw. There were two of them: one obese female, one obese male. He'd read their name-tags: Doris for the week days, Don on Saturdays and as a substitute. Both Doris and Don waved back.

He liked to watch the birds. Cardinals, bluejays, wrens, doves. Purple martin scouts flew up boldly, almost in Jim's face, searching for their nests from the previous year, when the house stood vacant. Jim had put up two hummingbird feeders, but he'd knocked down the martin nests. He needed a place to sit.

On Thursdays, a woman rode down the road on a chestnut mare, the mare twisting her head as if to cry out to Jim of her pointless and uncomfortable life, the woman with tall black boots, an upright quirt, and an upright back. She didn't belong here. She belonged in some old book if anywhere. This was hillbilly country, and the land remained stubborn despite the money outsiders threw down. Sooner rather than later, the woman would return to whatever fancy place she hailed from.

Kitty, Jim's daughter, had banished him to this old place, the home place, and the long porch Jim built twenty years ago. They didn't get along so well. Jim knew Kitty blamed him for divorcing

Sharon, her mother. Perhaps also she blamed him for Sharon's death, which came not long after.

Jim lived with Kitty for two years after his stroke and fancied he helped her some. He shuffled about and did the cooking—tuna casseroles and chili and tossed salads. When they went out, he listened to her recitation of problems at work, about which he had little to say. Her problems seemed insoluble. He said, "It'll look different tomorrow," or even, "You can't save the world in just one day."

Kitty was a nurse-practitioner, a hospitalist down in Joplin, and at least she made good money. Her biggest problem was love. Of course, that was everyone's problem. Even Jim's, if he could remember so far back.

Kitty went through several boyfriends. Usually, they were gone before midnight, never to return, but one of them, an accountant named Steve, appeared on several mornings. Jim talked to Steve about fishing on Lake Stockton and the Kansas City Royals, and the man seemed affable, though shy and apologetic. Why did young people— well, the accountant was over fifty—assume that old farts such as Jim had never carried on an affair?

Last Thanksgiving, Marlene took stage. She spent the night several times before bringing in her clothes. She and Kitty left for work together, rumpled and weary-seeming in their blue scrubs.

Marlene had enormous breasts. One morning, she came out of the bedroom wearing a lowcut blouse, and Jim couldn't help but stare. Not from lust—or if he did stare from lust, it was from that primordial part of the brainstem that tells you when to breathe. Thinking it over, Jim believed he'd stared from amazement, as if Marlene were a sideshow attraction. Regardless, Jim was slow to avert his eyes.

"Dirty old man!" Marlene said.

The remark took a moment to comprehend. He wondered how Kitty would react when Marlene complained, which he supposed she would. He'd be happy to leave, if it came to that. He was sick of living in town, trying to be useful.

Over chili, Kitty remembered how, when she was still a teenager, he'd take her out for dinner and flirt with the waitresses. "I was so embarrassed," she said.

He was lonely in those days. The waitresses flirted right back and maybe some of them were lonely, too. The only dishonest thing about it was that he tipped them well, as if he were an important man and his pockets were filled with money.

Maybe, in Kitty's estimation, he'd always been a dirty old man. She stammered and couldn't meet his eyes, finally suggesting he might be more comfortable living at the home place for a while. "You're a lot healthier now," she explained.

"Much healthier." The phrase that popped into his head was, "don't want to be a burden." This was his widowed mother's phrase, and Jim would pat her hand and say, "You're not a burden, Ma. You do all kinds of stuff for me."

The home place was perfect.

Two weeks later, Kitty brought out five boxes of groceries and a beagle pup, whom she'd already named Lucky. "Dad, I'm sorry," she said, looking at him with those unsteady eyes. "Marlene is—"

Jim cut her off. "Don't worry about it, Kitty. All you did was throw me into the briar patch."

Jim had owned beagles before. They were affectionate and loyal, but they were also clumsy and loved to dig holes everywhere. When he was a young man, Jim might have kept Lucky in the barn, but he needed a pal. So Lucky had the run of the old house, even upstairs where Jim's weak legs wouldn't allow him to go. Lucky ate Jim's food. He slept with the old man.

In April, Jim sat on the porch with Lucky in his lap. The day was warm and a breeze blew through the lilacs like an elixir. The mail ran and Jim waved at Doris/Don. He sat a while longer, mustering his strength, but he could walk half a mile now if he stopped to rest several times.

He hadn't seen the fancy woman on her chestnut mare and he missed her, but today there was another distraction. The Lamar girls' track team trotted by, their ponytails bobbing.

The beagle seized this moment to leap off Jim's lap and run to the road. He scurried about, falling down over his feet, yapping at the strange human machine of thrashing legs. With his littleness and floppy ears, Lucky was close to irresistible to tenderhearted young females, and they cooed and cried, "Aw" and "What a cutie." But they kept their formation—except for one.

Laughing, the girl bent low.

Jim had begun his slow walk down the driveway, but he understood he wasn't quick enough to capture the pup and dropped into a strategically placed lawn chair. He called out, "Lucky! Don't bother that girl!"

Lucky kept yapping. Sometimes, his terrier-like yap went deep, hinting at the sonorous, sonic boom of a bay not far in his future. He crawled on his belly toward the girl, and probably he'd follow her all the way to Nirvana. She picked up the pooch, kissed his nose, then ran to the lawn chair, delivering four sprawling paws into Jim's arms.

"Sorry," Jim said. "Lucky's a great little dog, he really is. But I started out for the mail and, you know, he's so full of energy."

"I'll get your mail for you, sir."

The girl raced to his mailbox with long strides. He thought of that graceful mare the proud lady rode.

The girl trotted back. "You're Jim Colson," she said.

He nodded. His name was on the mailbox.

"I'm Laura Penner. My mom brought me by here for Trick or Treat."

"I remember," Jim murmured. It wasn't a happy time, merely different, and those squirming urchins were indistinguishable. Sharon passed out apples from their Jonathan until a little old man came by, wearing a Marine Corps baseball hat and with a New Testament in his shirt pocket. He said apples could be poisoned and there was an ordinance against them.

"An ordinance against apples?" Sharon said.

"It's these times we're livin' in, Ma'am. In my opinion, these is the Last Days."

"I get it: apples are evil," Sharon said. "We're livin' in the Garden of Eden!"

They shut off the lights then, rather than pass out that Walmart treacle. There was your poison. Jim grinned, as he often did to memories, and was slow to realize that the track star was still talking to him.

"Come see us run, Mr. Colson," she said. "We're really fast!"

Wonderful. He'd been invited somewhere. But he visualized that huge parking lot, how far it was to those hard bleachers, how far back again to a port-a-potty, and knew he'd never watch the girl compete. "I will, Laura. You bet."

She smiled gently and Jim felt inspired. The country still produced innocent, wholesome girls.

But here was the patriotic question: Could you educate those girls so that they led happy lives? Could those girls ever be happier than they were at this ignorant moment, chattering about their teachers, their boyfriends, and ridiculous pop stars? And . . . what could he have done for Kitty so she turned out happier? Could he, weak and outmoded, a dirty old man, do something now?

Jim closed his eyes for a long time, as if the years would drop away and this old place could be a farm again. He seemed to hear corn rustling across the road, and hogs banging their snouts against their feeders. When he opened his eyes, the world had gone quiet, and the beagle played with a bug in a spot of sunshine.

In early May, Doris the mail carrier delivered one hundred Leghorn chicks in a flat box with breathing holes in the lid. Jim carried them out to the sagging barn and released them in the long concourse where he'd parked the Oliver tractor years before.

He'd already set up a brooder stove with chicken wire around it, so the idiot chicks couldn't burn themselves, and placed another ring of chicken wire, twenty feet across, around the stove. The Leghorns were helpless fluffs for the moment and wouldn't run much except to try to reach the heat.

He sat, day after day, with the radio on to the Kansas City Royals. He read slowly from an old book about the decline and fall of the Roman Empire. It had set on the mantel since he was a boy.

In three weeks, when the chicks showed pinfeathers, Jim climbed a straight ladder and washed off the dirt from two windows. The chicks ran back and forth in the sunshine, cheeping mightily, the little flock swerving in the long concourse, splitting into two streams at the tractor, piling up. Jim dragged a chair where the stove had been and sat with Lucky, who wasn't a pup anymore. When the dog wanted to leap down and chase the chicks, Jim held him back. "Nope," Jim said. "Don't need you chasin' our chickens."

In another two weeks, pullets writhed around Jim's ankles, and he set the dog down. The pullets stared cock-eyed at the dog, who walked peacefully among them. That night, Jim left Lucky in the barn, and at two in the morning Jim heard a baying that might or might not be Lucky's warning to a possum. In the morning, no harm had come to the pullets.

His leghorns would begin to lay at seventeen weeks. There was plenty of lumber around in the several buildings, and Jim brought it in a board at a time, and began building nests in what had been the feed room. It was difficult holding up the boards though he could drive nails all right. He drove two or three, then rested his arms.

"Dad!"

Kitty hadn't visited for several months, though she e-mailed him regularly. She tried to call but he never carried the phone. He shuffled down near the Oliver and sat on an overturned bucket. His chickens gathered around like an audience.

"Layers?" Kitty asked. "What will you do with the eggs?"

"Give you some. Sell the rest."

She smiled. "You won't get rich that way."

"The other thing is, I wonder if I could give you some money, and you could bring me in a battery for the Oliver."

"Sure, but—"

"And then we'll need to hook up the disk; it's out there in those pokeweeds."

"Why, Dad?"

"Wanna raise tomatoes. Wanna raise a lot of tomatoes. Eggs, tomatoes—people will stop for those."

"People." Kitty nodded gently, like her mother used to. Once in a while, at least. "I understand."

"Went up to the Senior Center in Lamar. Sat in a big, soft chair with all those old folks in their own soft chairs. You know you're old whcn you sit around all day with a blanket over your knees. *Murder, She Wrote* was playing, and then *Matlock,* and then *Murder, She Wrote* again. This may not be hell, I said to myself. But it sure looks like purgatory."

"I can drive the tractor. It'll be fun. By the way, Dad—"

Lucky ambled up, whining happily, and threw his paws against Kitty's abdomen. He tried to pull himself into her lap. "He's so big now!"

"Lucky watches out for our chickens. By the way what?"

"Marlene left," Kitty said. "She found a job in Arizona."

He remembered Marlene, the woman with enormous breasts. Because of Marlene, he'd come home again. "She didn't seem very happy to me."

"No." Kitty glanced at him, then stared at the Oliver. She swallowed. "I don't believe she was, Dad."

Fly-Up-the-Creek

Amy Wright Vollmar

Rats have gnawed
my kayak's hull,
so I can't stray

into midstream —
I float with
vivid wood ducks

who peep and weave
away from me
into a cove

where the bluff unfolds
for waterfall
and a ribbon snake

is hunting frogs.
We all watch seeds
of cottonwood

riding on green.
A drowning buckeye
wishes me luck

so I scoop it free
but my luck is already
good enough —

just upriver,
the little green heron
stays for me.

Abandon

Amy Wright Vollmar

I lean close
to swirls of spring
as the sycamores do—

rooted in
the outflow bank
they dare to veer,

reflect on green
as year by year
they fling themselves

farther across
the living pool
until they know

no other way—
they give up grace
to touch the spring.

Byway

Amy Wright Vollmar

In early spring
you'll have to feel
your own way

down the bluff,
because no map
will help you

once you slip
below the rim.
Follow a whiff

of the bobcat's fur
as he stirs
inside a rabbit dream—

you'll find his cave.
Beneath his sleep
you'll meet a spring

melting leaf-rime,
mapping a trail
all of its own

in filaments
of sound on stone,
where the planet's

youngest leaves
wake and unfurl
into black-and-white

warbler's flute,
the whirl of wings
through juniper.

And now beware—
below that spring
you will be lost,

astray in strains
of so many rivulets
seeking the river,

so many waterfalls.

Ecology of the Ozarks: Framing a Critical Place Conscious Pedagogy through Ecological Literacy

Cathie English

"Part of living well involves developing a sustainable relationship with the natural world in which one's community is located. Understanding the biology of one's region, how that biology connects to local industry and agriculture, and the consequent biological issues that impact one's community is thus a fundamental aspect of the ability to live well."

> Robert E. Brooke
> *Rural Voices: Place-Conscious Education*
> *and the Teaching of Writing*

My first understanding of a critical place conscious pedagogy with an ecological lens began in 1997 when I was first introduced to the concept of place-based education in a Nebraska Writing Project Rural Summer Institute. I formed my place conscious pedagogy upon Haas and Nachtigal's (1998) *Place Value: An Educator's Guide to Good Literature on Rural Lifeways, Environments, and Purposes of Education*, a thin volume, but one rich in the idea of instilling five senses into our students: a sense of place or living well ecologically; a sense of connection, or living well spiritually; a sense of worth or living well economically; a sense of belonging or living well in community; and a sense of civic involvement or living well politically. Instilling all these senses is important, and as a secondary English teacher, I focused upon four of the senses with some success. I exposed students to place-conscious texts: we read and annotated and discussed the arguments or themes of writers like Wendell Berry (2003), Wes Jackson (1996), Paul Gruchow (1995), and Derek Owens (2001). My students grasped their senses of connection, worth, civic involvement, and belonging through community literacy and ethnographic projects in a rural school in central Nebraska.

Despite my desire to emphasize how to live well ecologically, I never quite formulated the questions I needed to ask about how to instill a sense of place, or how I might move my students to grasp how crucial it was to sustain the soil, water, air, flora, and fauna of our locale. The current climate crisis has elicited a sense of urgency in me that has motivated me to further explore the questions of how we live well ecologically and instill a sense of place in our students. For the past eight years as an English/language arts (ELA) teacher educator, I have also asked myself, "How do I frame ecological literacy in our undergraduate and graduate students and how do I model this ecological literacy for pre-service and in-service ELA teachers so that they might enact ecological literacy in their future and present classrooms?"

Environmental educators have noted the difficulty of instilling a sense of place or teaching ecological literacy. Jo-Anne Ferreira (2019) states that over the past 50 years environmental education has not elicited the changes in human behavior that environmental educators had hoped to instill. She writes that educators need to shift their thinking and focus upon fashioning environmental citizens through immersion in nature, teaching environmental values, and focusing upon consumption practices and everyday impacts—ordinary experiences as common as washing dishes. She advocates for a sense of place meditation where learners "'make the connection between the problems of the entire planet and this one special place they have begun to value. The more they get to know the place, the more they will respect and remember one small place of the natural systems of our permanent home: Earth'" (p. 326).

Ruyu Hung (2017) names a sense of ecological literacy, ecophilia, "which means the human affective and embodied bond with other living beings and the environs, e.g., nature and place" (p. 43). Hung believes that to be ecologically literate, one must be able to "read, write, and calculate, but also being able to 'observe nature with insights, a merger of landscape and mindscape'" (p. 54). Kopnina and Saari (2019) raise the question about effective activism and engaged citizenship in environmental education and argue for the "need for reformed democracy and inclusive pluralism that recognizes the needs of nonhuman species, ecocentrism, and deep ecology" (p. 283). In a study of teachers' levels of ecological citizenship, Karatekin (2019) found that although teachers' environmental attitudes were fine-tuned, they had not participated in environmental activities, and he writes, "These results show us that ecological citizenship education should . . . increase the level of curiosity of individuals toward the environment and enable them to participate more in environmental activities" (p. 56).

My research of ecological literacy with both undergraduate and graduate students has revealed that many students have rarely been exposed to the concept of "ecology" throughout their K-12 or college or university experiences. During the summers of 2019 and 2020, I taught a summer intersession course, *Place Conscious Reading and Writing: Ecology of the Ozarks*, a mixed credit course that encompassed several principles of a critical place conscious pedagogy emphasizing inquiry into the ecology of a geographical place. In 2019, we took field trips to Hawksbill Crag in northwest Arkansas and the Missouri State Biological Field Station at Bull Shoals Lake; however, in Summer 2020, due to the COVID-19 pandemic, students conducted their own field trips to outdoor spaces of their choice. Except for Barbara Kingsolver's ecologically focused *Flight Behavior*, and Aldo Leopold's *Sand County Almanac*, an ecological literacy primer, I selected texts and excerpts that were based in the Ozarks, or written by Ozarkian writers focused upon ecological concepts: Sue Hubbell's *A Book of Bees: And How to Keep Them*; Ken Carey's *Flat Rock Journal: A Day in the Ozarks Mountains*; William B. Edgar, et al.'s *Living Ozarks: The Ecology and Culture of a Natural Place*; Phillip Howerton's *The Literature of the Ozarks: An Anthology*; Kenneth Smith's *The Buffalo River Handbook*; Amy Wright Vollmar's "Noland Hollow"; and Anthony Priest's *Yonder Mountain: An Ozarks Anthology*.

To better understand how to frame a critical place conscious ecological literacy, I collected data from this course including student writing, final reflections, final projects, and a survey. The students enrolled in the course included those majoring in English education, literature, creative writing, professional and technical writing, interdisciplinary studies, philosophy, biology, and political science. Over half the students were graduate students. At the beginning of this course, to gain insight into their ecological literacy and awareness, I conducted a survey that included the following:

• Which type of school and community best represents your K-12 educational experience? (Figure 1).

• Select any course work or field trip you may have experienced related to ecology in your K-12 educational experience (Figure 2).

• Select any course work or field trip you may have experienced related to ecology in your higher education or college educational experience (Figure 3).

• Describe your experience with any ecologically based course(s) throughout your K-16 (elementary, middle school, high school, and college) educational experience.

• Describe your experience with any ecologically based "enrichment" course(s) outside your K-16 (elementary, middle school, high school, and college) educational experience.

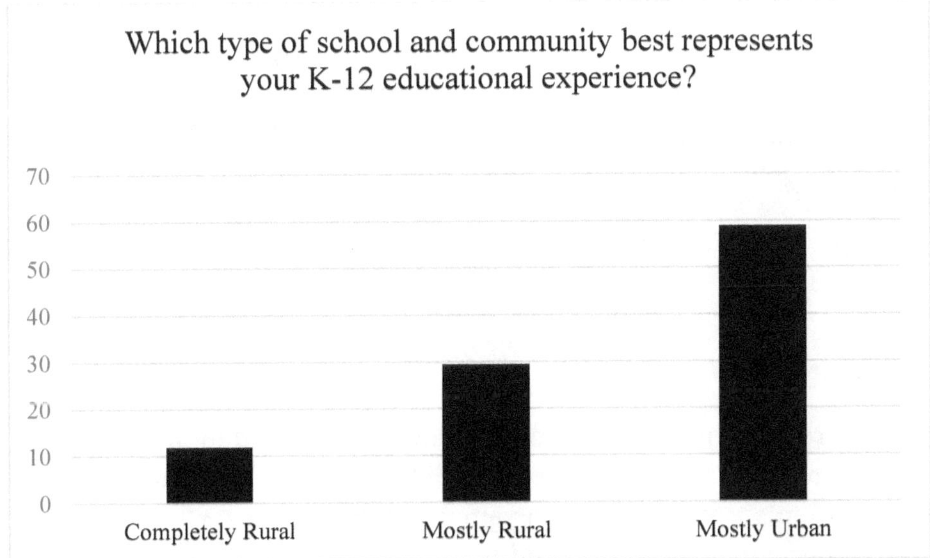

Figure 1.

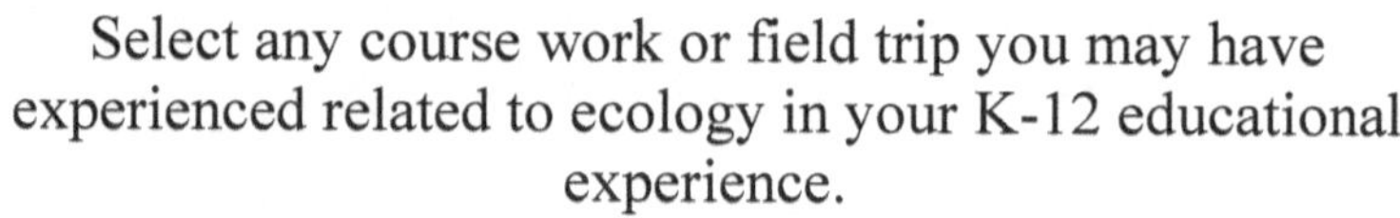

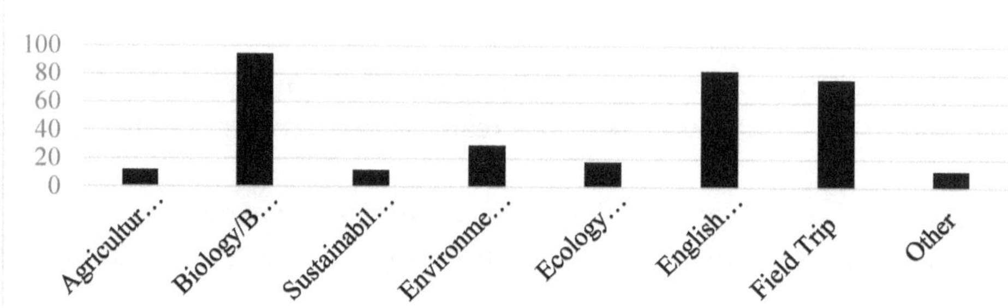

Figure 2.

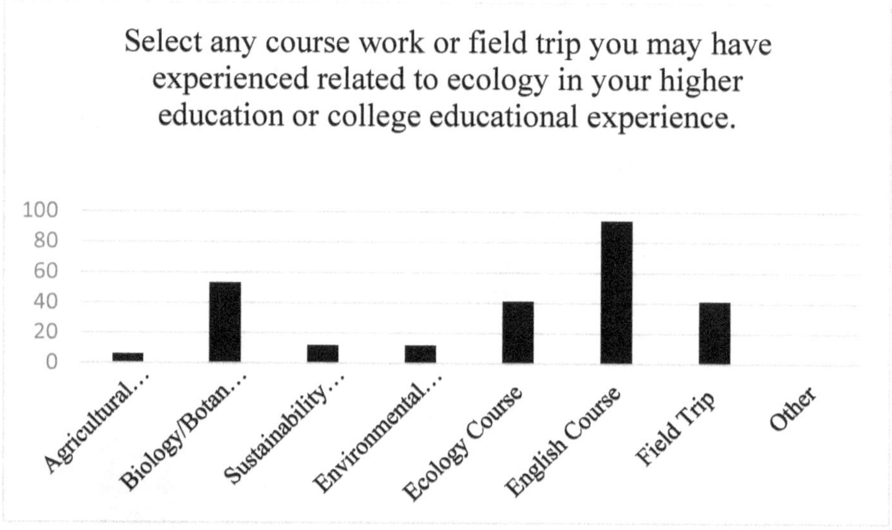

Figure 3.

It surprised me that most of the students enrolled in the course were from urban locations. Teaching in the Ozarks, I expected many more students from surrounding smaller communities, who lived in rural or remote areas who would have participated in agriculture programs. I assumed many might have taken horticulture classes with an emphasis in ecological awareness or some form of conservation education. Most students were exposed to the concept of ecological literacy in science programs; in fact, in their K-12 educations, 94% had experienced some form of ecological literacy in their biology or botany courses. This experience dropped off in the college experiences, though, to 54%. My interpretation of that statistic is that most college students have a wider choice of courses in fulfilling their general education science requirements, so some didn't take a biology course. What was striking to me is that 94% of students experienced some form of ecological literacy in English courses in college, but that may be because they included the current course in their responses. I wasn't expecting 82% of the students to have experienced some form of ecological literacy in English classes in K-12, but when I considered that more than half the students were from urban school districts, it occurred to me that some of them may have chosen electives that focused upon eco-criticism or eco-feminism or had teachers who were ecologically minded citizens. Just *under* half of the students in their K-12 experience had been enrolled in either an ecology or environmental course, while just over half had those experiences in higher education. Only 11% of the students at both the K-12 and higher education levels had taken a sustainability course.

Because experiential learning is a vital component of ecological awareness, I asked the question about field trips. Wattchow and Brown (2011) argue that place can be a source of identity, that an interaction with a place constructs and reconstructs one's identity:

> Outdoor places, like home places, have a vital role to play in the development and sustenance of identity. These places are always produced via a set of complex human-land interactions that is larger than the individual. Outdoor places need to be approached with a sense of humility: What happened here? Who has lived here? How have they lived? What seems to be happening to this place now—how is it changing? What is my role in that change? (71).

It was certainly encouraging to me that over three-fourths of the students had had some form of experiential learning through a field trip in their K-12 educations. Only 41% had some form of field trip as college students, and from my own experience coordinating field experiences for these students, I understand some of the obstacles, student transportation, and safety as the main concerns. Before our trip to Hawksbill Crag, I met with our university's legal counsel to craft a consent form because in April of 2018, a student from Briar Cliff University in Sioux City, Iowa, fell 100 feet to her death taking a selfie while on a field trip sponsored by the university. As faculty I was also responsible for coordinating student lodging, but that was simpler because of the field station where housing was provided. Field trips also require expert guides, and I was fortunate to have avid and expert hiker, Nancy Probstfeld from Reed Spring, Missouri, as our guide at Hawksbill Crag (and of whom one student wrote the following in a reflection of the trip): "Nancy was a great guide . . . she was clearly an expert on navigating the terrain and dealing with the differing seasons in the area, and I loved her sense of humor." Dr. Janice Greene, professor of biology and director of the Bull Shoals Field Station, was our expert guide who shared knowledge about field research, Bull Shoals Lake, and ornithological expertise about native bird species.

In response to the survey prompt "Describe your experience with any ecologically based course(s) throughout your K-16 (elementary, middle school, high school, and college) educational experience," most students conveyed they had not had many formal experiences in the classroom with an ecological lens. One student wrote, "Aside from receiving a tree on Arbor Day 1981, none." Others wrote of being in an ecology club and taking an environmental science class focused on nonfiction and research. Some wrote about field trips to Wilson's Creek, the Springfield Conservation Nature Center, Fantastic Caverns, area farms, picnics, caves, caverns, streams, rivers, and woods. Some of these students noted there was no specific class at that time in their secondary schools; science class was their only exposure to ecological literacy. One student wrote, "I have loved science (environmental especially) since I was in the sixth grade. Science class was one of my favorites in school always." The biology major/sustainability minor student noted that his or her entire schooling included ecologically based courses; they had taken field trips to Springfield Lake and to the Watershed Center. They also did some volunteering for a class where they helped the local Springfield Community Gardens. Another student noted they had grown up in a completely rural area and that they and their peers were all farm kids whose parents ran their own greenhouses. Most students' experiences in ecological literacy were limited, but not all. One student wrote the following:

> I remember learning about watersheds and taking a trip to a nearby river when I was in Elementary school. My teacher taught us about the ecosystem of the river, and we did a lot of hands-on learning on that field trip. Later in my K-12 education I took a biology course, and we did several labs during the class. I did engage in the environment to some degree in my K-12 years . . . In college we did so much more with the environment. I took a Utopian criticism class where we traveled to a nearby intentional community and learned about their sustainable relationship with the environment . . . I also helped found a 'Hiking Club' at Missouri State-West Plains.

In their response to the survey prompt "Describe your experience with any ecologically based "enrichment" course(s) *outside* your K-16 (elementary, middle school, high school, and college) educational experience," just over half of the students commented that they had no enrichment classes outside of their K-16 experiences. One student wrote that while in middle and high school, they participated in science fairs and that all their projects had to do with the environment. Several students noted their own personal engagements with the environment, noting they liked exploring places and going to museums or "creating a course for yourself" or going to many of the natural areas throughout the Ozarks. One student wrote, ". . . when I travel somewhere new, I . . . partake in a 'mini-course' where people who are familiar with an area or place share history and information about it . . . even if they are really just a snapshot of the place I am visiting or discovering." Other students wrote about their immersion in nature because they grew up on farms. Two students had experienced ecology-based summer camps during middle school that included hikes, scuba diving, and environmental and sustainability courses taught through Disney University. One urban student had participated in creative writing workshops through The Writers Place in Kansas City, Missouri. These workshops focused upon "place" and sometimes included walks on nature trails and local neighborhoods. Another student taught summer school for 2nd and 3rd graders, focused upon teaching sustainability.

Over the three-week intersession course, students were asked to complete a culminating project of their choice, depending upon their academic major. Both undergraduate and graduate English education students could choose to create a text set and rationale for teaching a unit focused upon ecological literacy. They were to provide a brief description of the texts they might use and an explanation of how these texts help them address the specific needs of their students. They were also asked to craft a "launching lesson," the initial lesson of their unit that serves as a hook for the entire unit. Creative writing or professional writing majors could choose to compose in one or more genre, including fiction, poetry, or creative non-fiction. Their writing could draw upon the writing during our field trips to Hawksbill Crag and to the Bull Shoals Field Station. I asked them to consider what they might write from an ecological perspective. Literature students were guided to craft a literary analysis of one of the course texts, considering a theoretical perspective to focus upon as they crafted their analysis. Of course, any student in any major was free to select any of these options. In 2019, students chose widely from these options, e.g., literary analyses of novels and poems, a proposal, short stories, poetry, and text sets and rationales. However, in the summer of 2020, only one student wrote a literary analysis; most students wrote poetry or creative non-fiction. I attributed this to the pandemic and our online modality and one of our guest speakers on Zoom, poet Amy Wright Vollmar. Vollmar's candid conversations about her poetry elicited many meaningful questions and responses and inspired poetry writing from students.

Writing about our place is an integral part of this *Ecology of the Ozarks* course. In 2019, students sat near the edges of Hawksbill Crag (but not too close as I admonished them) and observed the forest and skies and wrote in their journals. At Bull Shoals Field Station, we conducted a writing marathon which included movement from one place or space to another over several hours, culminating in a read aloud held at Kim's BBQ Shack in Kirbyville, Missouri, not far from the field station. Participants consult with their writing group members and select one of their pieces from the marathon for the read-aloud. Over several years of writing marathon experiences, I have witnessed the phenomenon of poetry; that is, when writers are in nature, they have a predilection to write poetry. And our exposure to Bull Shoals Lake was no exception:

High Water on Bull Shoals Lake

Shimmering ripples of blueish-green and white,
gliding in unison, carrying debris,
wind and fate acting as its guide.

The driftwood, remnants of yesterday's land,
Cast out and repurposed,
Finding its place on the glassy surface.

On the shore, displaced limbs and brush
lay scattered in piles,
now home to happy residents.

Untitled

Morning slowly making an exit
Sun reaching its peak
Trees shadowing like a royal canopy
As beams make an appearance through branches and leaves

Close your eyes and listen
Let the call of nature fill your ears
Allow the birds to serenade you
For a free concert is always nice

Eliminate all distractions
Let yourself be pulled in
Nature has a way with NO words

You can say it's like a picture

Listen for the whistle of the wind
As it carries your soul into the woods
Tomorrow you'll be a new person
For you've been reborn by the wind

In 2020, because of COVID restrictions, we didn't travel to Hawksbill Crag or Bull Shoals, but I requested that students conduct their own individualized field trips, and I suggested the following: hiking a trail, sitting in your backyard, tending your garden, strolling the Springfield Conservation Nature Center or Nathaniel Greene Park, visiting some other local or a state park, or kayaking a lake or stream. I asked them to think about what they observed and to keep a field guide where they could write or draw plants, flowers, or animals. I wanted to know what they learned about this landscape/geographical area. Once again, I wasn't surprised to witness the poetry phenomenon on full display:

In My Own Backyard

Grass covers the ground
Like a bright green carpet
So soft
you want to rub your cheek against it.

Bright red male cardinal warns his mate
And bluejay antagonizes
Until a woodpecker interrupts the dispute
To drill for a snack.
Birds of all colors
Fly in and out of trees
The perfect habitat for their nests.

A moss covered stump sits nearby
Filled with purple wildflowers
A soft reminder

In death, grows new life.

Trees sprinkled here and there
Offering the perfect amount of shade
And mosquitos.
To the east, a garden
Bordered by wire fencing
And wooden boards.
It waits to be filled
With this year's crops.

Chickens peck the ground at a nearby woodpile
Searching for bugs
From last night's rain.
They fear no daytime predator
In their backyard oasis.

I ask students to write a reflection at the end of the course highlighting their experiences, as a means for me to rethink and revise my curriculum choices, to gain a better understanding of what I may have missed or points of oversight. All students wrote compelling reflections about the reading and writing and field trip experiences, but one student's response stood out:

> My experience with Place Conscious Reading and Writing was one that I will cherish not only as a means through which I learned about a particular region, but in that I have learned a new way to view and approach areas where I live and travel. This class has awakened in me a greater awareness of the spaces and places around me as well as a deeper curiosity and appreciation for landscapes and even ecosystems near and far. Learning about a region through the lens of its ecology was fascinating; it revealed a new angle to not only take in and learn about my surroundings, but also allowed me to discover more about myself in terms of my interests for readings and passions for writing.

This student's response reflects the beginning of an ecological literacy I hope will continue for a lifetime—it will take our lifetimes and beyond to sustain the ecosystem of the Ozarks. This response echoes the words of David Orr (2005) about the importance of inhabiting a place:

> The study of place has . . . a significance in reeducating people in the art of living well where they are. The distinction between inhabiting and residing is important here . . . A resident is a temporary occupant . . . The inhabitant, in contrast, "dwells" in "an intimate, organic and mutually nurturing relationship with a place". . . . A place has a human history and a geologic past; it is part of an ecosystem with a variety of microsystems, it is a landscape with a particular flora and fauna. Its inhabitants are part of a social, economic, and political order. (p. 92)

Over the past nine years, I've come to dwell in this place, the Ozarks, and every day, I'm in awe of its unique ecosystem. I walk trails and take photos of native species, so I can learn their names and study their habits. I have come face to face with confused and panicked deer who are now being displaced due to increased subdivision development. I sit on the banks of Wilson's Creek and listen to the water rush over the rocks and investigate the nature of these rocks to understand the geology of this place and how that knowledge can teach me about a place over a millennium. At night, I listen to the coyote and owl. David Orr, too, came to inhabit the Arkansas Ozarks when he created an environmental education center, Meadowcreek, where students could come and learn on the 1,500 acres. He writes of his own experience here that "opened the door to the different possibility that education ought, somehow, to be more of a dialogue requiring the capacity to listen to the wind, water, animals, sky, nighttime sounds, and what [indigenous people] once described as earthsong" ("Recollection," p. 104).

My future investigation of ecological literacy will include what David Greenwood names "decolonization soul work" or a cosmological homecoming, something he believes is crucial in understanding of place *as land* and a necessary critique of settler colonialism (p. 371). Greenwood cites Lilburn who asks all of us to "learn more about who we are, where we came from, and why we are in this place. These are our origin stories; they are cosmic, geographical, cultural and political; they tell us what and where home is" (p. 375). Scott Russel Sanders writes that it took him half his lifetime to understand how to live a grounded life, searching and traveling to find his spiritual center. His epiphany was that he must be grounded in the "land itself, with its creeks and rivers, its weather, seasons, stone outcroppings, and all the plants and animals that share it. I cannot have a spiritual center without having a geographical one; I cannot live a grounded life without being grounded in a *place*" (pp.120-121).

How do I teach this kind of soul work when I have barely just begun to elicit a basic ecological literacy? I'm still a newcomer to the Ozarks. I'm still learning. For me, this kind of grounding work is the ecological literacy of translation. My goal will be to learn and teach an interpretative language of translation so my students will understand how to translate the earthsongs—the language of the lake, the crag, the creek, and the cave. Over the course of two summers, my students demonstrated a language of translation as poetry. Together, we will translate our own cosmological homecoming stories, and to "never live someone else's story, but to live as well as we can, our own story of being and becoming, and to learn to give this story voice, in the presence of others, wherever we find ourselves" (Greenwood, p. 375).

References

Berry, W. (2003). Going to work. *Citizenship Papers*. Shoemaker and Heard.

Brooke, R. (Ed.). (2003). *Rural voices: Place-conscious education and the teaching of writing* (Vol. 25). Teachers College Press.

Carey, K. (1994). *Flat rock journal: A day in the Ozark mountains*. Harper San Francisco.

Edgar, W. B., Besara, R. M., & Baumlin, J. S. (2018). *Living Ozarks: The Ecology and Culture of a Natural Place*. Ozarks Studies Institute of Missouri State University.

Ferreira, J. A. (2019). The limits of environmental educators' fashioning of 'individualized' environmental citizens. *The Journal of Environmental Education, 50*(4-6), 321-331.

Greenwood, D. A. (2019). Place, land, and the decolonization of the settler soul. *The Journal of Environmental Education, 50*(4-6), 358-377.

Gruchow, P. (1995). *Grass roots: The universe of home*. Milkweed.

Haas, T., & Nachtigal, P. (1998). *Place value: An educator's guide to good literature on rural lifeways, environments, and purposes of education*. ERIC Clearinghouse.

Howerton, P. D. (Ed.). (2019). *The literature of the Ozarks: An anthology*. University of Arkansas Press.

Hubbell, S. (1998). *A book of bees: And how to keep them*. Houghton Mifflin Harcourt.

Hung, R. (2017). Towards ecopedagogy: An education embracing ecophilia. *Educational Studies in Japan, 11*, 43-56.

Jackson, W. (1996). Matfield green. In W. Vitek & W. Jackson (Eds.), *Rooted in the land: Essays on community and place* (pp. 95-103). Yale University Press.

Karatekin, K. (2019). Model review related to the effects of teachers' levels of ecological citizenship. *International Electronic Journal of Environmental Education, 9*(1), 46-61.

Kingsolver, B. (2012). *Flight behavior*. Faber & Faber.

Kopnina, H., & Saari, M. H. (2019). If a tree falls: Business students learning active citizenship from environmentalists. *Education Sciences, 9*(4), 284.

Leopold, A. (1989). *A Sand County almanac, and sketches here and there.* Oxford University Press, USA.

Orr, D.W. (2005). Place and pedagogy. In M.K. Stone & Z. Barlow (Eds.), *Ecological literacy: Educating our children for a sustainable world* (pp. 85-96). North Atlantic Books.

Orr, D.W. (2005). Recollection. In M.K. Stone & Z. Barlow (Eds.), *Ecological literacy: Educating our children for a sustainable world* (pp. 96-106). North Atlantic Books.

Owens, D. (2001). *Composition and sustainability: Teaching for a threatened generation.* National Council of Teachers of English

Priest, A. (Ed.). (2013). *Yonder mountain: An Ozarks anthology.* University of Arkansas Press.

Sanders, S. R. (1993). *Staying put: Making a home in a restless world.* Beacon Press (MA).

Smith, K. L. (2004). *Buffalo river handbook.* University of Arkansas Press.

Vollmar, A.W. (2019, March 25). Noland hollow. *Elder mountain: A journal of Ozarks studies.* 9.

Wattchow, B., & Brown, M. (2011). *A pedagogy of place: Outdoor education for a changing world.* Monash University Publishing.

The Idea of Order in Arkansas

Terrell Tebbetts

"…for here was a woman with a civilizing mission."
Junot Díaz in *The Brief and Wonderous Life of Oscar Wau*

"Please don't tell my mama" peals again
from Mikey's puckered mouth—
as when at five he did a Mondrian
with scavenged paint, the neighbors' new-laid brick
inviting like a canvas, or when at six
he aimed his broomstick bat at hanging ferns
enticing him along another neighbor's porch.

But now, at nine, he's practiced war
by lobbing rock grenades at Gracie when
she pedaled past his cardboard fort.

"Please don't tell my mama!"

Yet every time his plea has fallen flat,
for Mama's heard, and then while Daddy's
bagging ducks or stalking deer
or scoping out wild turkey, Mama's
marched her noble savage to the scene
of malefaction to see that he atones
with wadded birthday dollars, downcast eyes,
and murmurs of apology—to learn,
she's hoped, the self-restraint that saves
us from a Hobbesian collapse.

This time, as Mikey turns to trudge back home,
apology complete, he seems like David
being sculpted from our Ozark clay,
Mama scooping out the flaws
till every excess splatters to the floor,
to manifest at last magnificence
which only she now sees.

Extra Innings

Michelle Collins Anderson

Jenna and her brother Boo belted out "Ninety-Nine Bottles of Beer" in the back seat of the Pontiac station wagon on the way to the Murphy family's first-ever Cardinal baseball game. Boo — not quite three and unable to count backwards — screamed the chorus at the top of his lungs: Take one down, pass it around! At ninety-one bottles, their dad barked from the driver's seat: "Put a lid on it, Pork Chop."

Jenna almost said, "Put a bottle cap on it," but she could see her dad was already mad about something. His brown eyes were almost black as he glanced from the rearview mirror to her mother, whom he called "Doodle" because she was such a scatterbrain. In Jenna's family, there were lots of nicknames. Jenna was "Pork Chop," even though she didn't like pork chops at all, or even bacon. Her dad made "Pork Chop" sound sweet, but Jenna had the feeling he was making fun of her for something she couldn't help: she had always been plain and a little pudgy. Meanwhile, her brother "Boo-Boo" or "Boo" (was it possible to have a nickname for a nickname?) had been a "mistake," according to her dad, although her mother shushed him when he said that. Even the station wagon — a long yellow banana of a car flanked by dark wooden paneling — was dubbed the "Big Bruiser." Her father was just "Dad" to Jenna and Boo and "Joe" to her mother. But then, Jenna knew he couldn't be expected to give a nickname to himself. She was only eight, but she knew that wasn't how things worked.

"Did you see how they looked at me?" Her father's eyes were fixed on her mother instead of the road. "That idiot brother-in-law of yours, all tight-lipped at lunch. Mr. Know-It-All. And did you hear your sister? 'There's the couch for you, Joe.' Jesus Christ, what did you tell them?"

Jenna's mother swiped beneath the bottom rims of her sunglasses with her fingers. She looked glamorous and mysterious with her sunglasses on. Usually she wore them on top of her head, where she often forgot she had them on at all.

"Just ignore it, okay? But," she added, as if she couldn't stop herself, "what was I supposed to tell them? That everything was hunky-dory?"

"You called me, remember?" Jenna's dad glowered a long few seconds before turning his eyes back to the road.

Her mom looked out the window, her long pale neck ending in dark, short hair with little curls, like commas, in front of her ears. She wore a sleeveless white blouse and a denim wraparound skirt because she didn't have anything red to wear to the game.

"Do I look pretty to you?" she had asked Jenna, posing in the floor length mirror at Aunt Mena and Uncle Ted's before they left for the game. Jenna said yes, but her mother kept pulling at her blouse and skirt. She leaned in close to the mirror and traced her mouth with bright red lipstick. Then she smacked her lips open and closed like a fish.

"There," she said, snapping the tube closed.

They had planned to stay at Jenna's aunt and uncle's after the game tonight because it was cheaper than a motel. Aunt Mena was her mom's sister who lived just outside St. Louis, hours away from the Murphys' little Ozarks town. Jenna's mom thought it would be nice to visit before the game and spend the night afterwards. Do something "touristy" together on Saturday.

But that was before the big fight.

One night three weeks ago, Jenna was dreaming that she had inched her way down the dark basement stairs and found herself squinting in the sun on an African savannah. A pride of hungry lions stared back at her. She froze, unable to move or scream. One lion shook his mane and opened his mouth, but instead of a roar, her father's voice came out in a terrible yell. Then Jenna came fully awake and padded on bare feet to her parents' room. She tried the doorknob but it wouldn't open. The shouting stopped and she heard her mother sobbing. Her dad opened the door angrily, as if expecting someone else.

"Go back to bed, Pork Chop."

"I had a bad dream." Jenna hugged her middle. Her mother was lying on the bed, facing away from the door, her back shuddering with each gulping breath. "Mama?"

"Your mom's fine. Go back to bed."

"I'm obviously not fine, Joe." Her mother rolled over and looked at Jenna with wet, puffy eyes. "Tell her what's wrong with me."

"There's nothing wrong with you, Doodle."

"No. Go ahead. I want to hear you say it." Jenna's mom sat up slowly, drawing her knees into her chest and reaching for a cigarette. Her hand shook and she knocked over a clutch of empty beer cans on the dresser.

"What the hell's with you?"

"That's right, tell her." She looked at Joe and put the cigarette to her lips. "Tell her how you don't love me anymore."

Joe gave an exasperated sigh and hefted Jenna to the middle of the bed. Her nightgown bunched up around her thighs, and the bright light from the single ceiling fixture hurt Jenna's eyes. It felt like she was in trouble, except she couldn't remember doing anything wrong.

Her dad exhaled loudly. "Okay. Here's the deal. You know your mom and I love you. And Boo. Right?" He seemed to be waiting for Jenna to respond, but her brain felt fuzzy and she couldn't figure out what he wanted her to say.

"Anyway. We've decided it's best if your mom and I aren't married anymore."

"Ha!" But her mother's laugh wasn't really a laugh. "Best for you and what's-her-name."

"Doodle, goddamn it. Don't. We said we'd make it nice. For the kids."

"I didn't agree to anything. To any of this." Jenna's mother's hands fluttered around her face like frantic white birds. "Remember that, Jenna. This is all your father."

Jenna looked from one angry face to the other. Her stomach hurt.

"Can I have some Chips Ahoy?" she asked, though the pain didn't feel like a hungry hurt.

Joe snorted. "That's my girl," he said. He swooped her off the bed and boosted her onto his shoulders, where she leaned precariously until he grasped her shins and righted her.

"C'mon, Pork Chop. Let's go get some cookies."

Over the next few days, there had been more loud, tearful arguments. One had to do with furniture: Jenna's mom did not want their bed anymore. She took it apart and dragged all the pieces out into the front yard like they were having a yard sale. Then, two days later, she pulled it all back inside, though she hadn't yet put the bed back together. She slept on the mattress on the floor, while Joe stayed on the couch.

The other fight was about money. Jenna got the idea that she and Boo were expensive, and that Joe didn't want to pay for them. Or pay enough. That one ended with Joe slamming the front door and driving off for a few hours. The next day Jenna had followed him around the house solemnly as he packed his clothes, shoes, shaving kit and radio into a black trash bag, its slick black surface distended with lumps and sharp edges.

"For Christ's sake, Pork Chop," he said, twisting the top of the bag in a half-effort to keep it closed. "You look like your best friend just died."

"How will I listen to the Cardinals without the radio?"

Joe squatted down to look her in the eyes. He reached one hand toward her cheek and pinched it, giving the chub of flesh a little shake. "It will be okay."

So things had gotten quieter at home. Jenna noticed it at the beauty shop where her mom worked, too. Her mom did hair on Friday afternoons and evenings and all day Saturday, so Jenna and Boo had to hang around until Joe got off work. They listened as her mom raged about Joe to the women who took turns in her chair, nodding their wet heads set in foils or giant pink curlers.

But after a while, Jenna began hearing something different in the beauty shop women's voices; a tone slightly needly under their words, like a splinter you can't see. Like they were more interested in Joe than her mom. Her mom must have heard it, too, because one night she told Jenna that it might be okay for Joe to come back.

"If he's really sorry," she said. "Because I do still love him. He may be an asshole, but he's my asshole."

Jenna didn't think that sounded like love, but she did want her dad back. So when her mom called Joe to suggest they take the trip to St. Louis after all, she was thrilled her dad said yes. He had already bought the four tickets and asked off from the garage where he worked, he said. And Jenna's mom had made the plans with her sister months ago.

"It's a chance to start over," Jenna overheard her mom say, as she pulled the dome of a dryer down over a customer's steel gray hair wrapped in purple plastic rollers.

"You two have to be really, really good," Jenna's mom said before Joe had picked them up for the drive to St. Louis. "No fighting or crying. No begging for stuff. Or peeing or pooping your pants," she added, with a sharp look at Boo.

Jenna felt hopeful inside, like she had swallowed a shiny bubble, floaty and beautiful.

The Big Bruiser was on Highway 40 now, and Jenna could see the Gateway Arch in the July haze, a silver rainbow with the tiniest of rectangular windows at the top. In an instant, the arch disappeared as the highway ducked beneath another, throwing the station wagon into shadow as they closed in on downtown. Joe braked as the traffic thickened and pulled the car sharply into the exit lane. Jenna's mother stiffened.

"I wish you'd watch where you're going," she said, gripping the door.

"See me getting into any accidents?" Joe sped up on purpose, braking at the last second at the bottom of the ramp. Boo rolled to the floor with a thump and started crying.

"Joe!" Jenna's mother reached through the gap in the front seats, feeling around for Boo behind her. "You're okay, baby."

Boo climbed back onto his seat, still blubbering. He had just started wearing "big boy pants." Jenna was glad because poopy diapers smelled awful. But now they spent lots of time in bathrooms.

Between her mother making Boo pee every hour and him loving the novelty of different restrooms, Jenna was pottied out.

Jenna saw a brown sign to Busch Stadium and then they were on a street lined with buildings so tall she had to tilt her head all the way back to see the tops.

"There's a parking lot." Jenna's mother pointed to a large hand-painted sign propped outside an asphalt lot. Her dad shook his head.

"I'm not paying ten bucks for parking," he said.

"But we've got the kids, water . . ." Her mother sighed. "Please. Let's not hike ten miles."

He kept driving until they came to a lot that was empty except for a broken-down car. Joe slammed his door closed and threw open the back of the station wagon; the rest of the family stretched and yawned. Jenna felt relieved to be out of the car. But she could not see Busch Stadium anywhere. Jenna knew they would all have to carry something, except Boo, who would himself be carried on their father's shoulders. She felt a stab of envy.

Her mother gripped a large straw purse and had the mint green diaper bag slung over one shoulder — with wipes and extra briefs — "just in case." She held Boo's hand as he stood blinking in the smoldering sunlight. The asphalt felt warm and sticky beneath Jenna's thin sandals, as if it had been liquid earlier in the afternoon. It wasn't that much cooler now. Jenna was glad she had on her sleeveless red top, the one that stretched over her sticky-out tummy with the matching polyester shorts that were just the slightest bit tight.

Joe unscrewed the lid from the dark green gallon jug and poured out an inch of water, careful not to spill the ice cubes floating on top.

"What are you doing?" Jenna's mother asked. "It's almost game time."

Joe reached into a Styrofoam cooler, grabbing an awkward fistful of beer cans. He dropped three into the depths of the jug, tightened the cap and handed the whole thing to Jenna.

"Come on. You're kidding, right?" Her mother was pleading half-heartedly, like she was already resigned to letting Joe have his way. "You're making your daughter sneak in your beer?"

"You don't seem to mind drinking it." He reached for the diaper bag and shoved two more cans beneath the clothes. Her mother's face clouded over, like she was making a hard decision. Finally, she lifted Boo under the armpits and placed him on Joe's shoulders.

"You kids ready to have some fun?"

It was a long walk. Jenna's mom and dad and Boo were out in front, while Jenna trudged behind, trying to match the slosh of the ice in the jug with the slap, slap of her sandals on the sidewalk. She thought what a nice picture the three of them made, her little brother a mix of her mother's dark hair and her dad's curls. She noticed her mother wind a finger through one of Joe's belt loops. Joe didn't look at her, but he didn't shake her off, either.

The hard plastic handle began to wear a blister on Jenna's hand. She tried to distract herself by thinking about the cotton candy her dad had promised her. Jenna had decided on pink.

"Ball!" Boo was pointing a finger at the ballpark stadium, which had just become visible as the Murphys crossed another street. They joined the crowds of people streaming toward the ballpark like salmon, their red t-shirted bellies and ball caps bouncing as they walked.

"That's right, Boo-Boo. Ball." Jenna's dad seemed happier, and her mom paused to let Jenna catch up. She took the water jug.

"Let me carry it for a while," she said, patting Jenna on the head while she smiled up at Joe. Jenna's sweating scalp had soaked her thin blond hair and her shorts were riding up. She tugged the stretchy material out of the crack of her bottom.

Jenna had seen Busch Stadium plenty of times on TV. From the aerial shots, it looked like a bundt pan or a hubcap, with scallops cut out of the top edge that showed the sky. But up close, it seemed more like a giant alien spaceship had landed in downtown St. Louis.

Her mom handed back the water right before they reached the ticket takers. Jenna pushed her way through the greasy metal bar of the turnstile. A man with a badge asked to see her mother's purse. He didn't touch the diaper bag. No one asked to see Jenna's water, either. Her dad smirked as he took the jug from her. Then he was walking faster up the cement ramp, a lightness in his gait, even with the added weight of the water and Boo still on his shoulders, grabbing Joe's thick blond hair in his fist like a saddlehorn.

Jenna scrambled to keep up. They went up and up and around and around in the breezeless heat, past impatient people lined up for last-minute snacks, past the beer booths and the t-shirt vendors. Jenna smelled buttered popcorn and stale beer; she heard the hiss of brats on a grill. Joe stopped to buy a scorecard, and Jenna spied a cotton candy booth where a stooped old man sat twirling a paper cone in a giant bowl. His apron was smeared with blue and pink. The man caught Jenna's eye and winked. She pulled at her dad's shirt, but he was already moving.

"Later, okay?"

Their seats were near the top of the upper deck overlooking third base. It was so high that the baseball field looked pretend, the size of a postcard. Jenna felt dizzy. Her dad set Boo down, and he scrambled into their row, folding down a seat. There was no one around them. Two rows farther up, an old man without any teeth sat eating popcorn. He nodded at Joe and gave Jenna's mom a smile that was mostly wet popcorn.

"We paid all that money for this?" Her mother surveyed the stadium through her large black sunglasses. Jenna could see herself in them, round and rumpled.

"C'mon. We're worth it."

Jenna's mom seemed to consider this. "I would have thought we were worth a little more."

"Sit down and have a cold one, why don't you? Pork Chop, hand me a beer." Jenna could tell her dad wasn't going to let her mom ruin his good mood. He plopped down beside Boo, while her mother pushed past Jenna to take the seat beside Joe, frowning.

Jenna sat next to her mom, the backs of her thighs sticking to the seat. She unscrewed the cap of the jug and fished around until she found a can, the icy water sending shooting pains up her arm. She reached across her mother's lap to place the beer in Joe's outstretched hand.

"Thanks, Porks."

The Star Spangled Banner started up, sounding tinnier this far away than it did on the radio. Joe stood, hand slapped over his heart. Jenna got up, too, but Boo and her mother just stayed put. The sun was setting, giving the arch a rosy pink glow above the stadium.

Jenna's mom sniffled quietly. "This is stupid."

"Just try to have a good time. For the kids, for Christ's sake."

"But what about me? What about us?" Jenna's mom's voice wavered. "If I had known this was all I would be missing, I would've let you have my ticket. God."

She sank back into her seat, but the air had gone out of her, like an old birthday balloon. She started to cry. "But then you would have taken her."

"I'm here with you now, aren't I?"

"Are you?"

"Doodle."

"Don't call me that."

Jenna's mom watched Joe with wet, hopeful eyes and seemed to be waiting for him to say something more. But he just took another long gulp of Bud and wiped his mouth on his t-shirt. Then he unfolded the scorecard and started filling in the lineups with the stunted, eraserless pencil that came with it. Boo climbed over him, reaching for his mother.

"Goddamn it, Boo. You're wrinkling my program."

"Be still," Jenna's mother warned Boo without much enthusiasm. She tried to force him to sit on her lap, but he arched against her. She let him slide out of her grasp. Boo, surprised to be free, stood unsteadily for a moment before starting toward the steep cement stairs.

"Can we get something to eat?" Jenna's mom asked.

"Already?" Joe grouched. "I told you I didn't bring a lot of cash. Christ! A leadoff double. Motherfu--."

"Joe! Please?"

He stuck the scorecard between his seat and one leg as he dug into the pocket of his jeans for a crumpled twenty. Joe tossed the bill toward Jenna's mom without even looking at her, like she was a waitress. Jenna's mom acted like she didn't notice. "What would you like, babe?" she asked. Jenna snapped her head around; she hadn't heard her mom call Joe that for weeks.

"I guess I'll have a Coke if you're going."

"Perfect. I'll take Boo." Her mother was already up three stairs when Jenna remembered.

"Can I have my cotton candy, Dad?" Jenna wasn't hungry yet, but she was worried they might run out of money. "Mama?"

Her mother stopped without turning around and sighed. "What color?"

"Pink."

Jenna considered going along. She didn't trust her mother to remember the right color, even after being told. But she didn't want to miss the game. Or being with her dad.

The Cardinals were playing the L.A. Dodgers, and Jenna knew a few of their players: Ron Cey, Bill Russell, and Steve Garvey. But she knew all the Cardinals by heart, and their stats, too. She had spent almost every evening of her summers sitting next to her dad on the couch, or outside on the porch swing, listening to Jack Buck and Mike Shannon do the play-by-play on the radio while her dad drank beer and offered his own commentary. He was unquestionably loyal to the Cardinals, but his affection for any one player was fickle and moody. He had a short memory when someone hit a rough patch. Jenna would argue to keep the faith in a reliever or hitter, but her dad would say "Yeah, but what has he done for me lately, Pork Chop?" He would pat her shoulder and call her his "devil's advocate," which sounded scary but important.

Jenna liked all the Cardinals, but if asked her favorite, she always said Lou Brock. He was a great leadoff hitter and could steal like crazy. He was humble, too, with a shy smile that made him seem as surprised as anybody when he put one over on the catcher or pitcher.

Secretly, though, Ted Simmons was her true favorite, but it felt naughty to like him. He wore No. 23 and had longish black hair and a bad temper. She read his lips on TV after he struck out; he was not "rated G" was how her mom put it. He knew lots of the same swear words as her dad, actually. She liked that he batted "clean up." You could rely on Ted Simmons — "Simba," her Dad called him — for an RBI when there were men on base. He could homer, too.

Jenna wished they had binoculars. She couldn't make out the players' faces like on TV. Her dad had finished his second beer and cracked open another after moving the lukewarm cans from the diaper bag to the water jug. "Come here, Pork Chop. Let me show you something."

Jenna moved into her mom's vacated seat while her dad smoothed out the scorecard with his hand, careful not to smudge the pencil marks. She saw the tiny baseball diamonds in every space. He showed her how to mark the double, carefully tracing the path from home to first to second. A ground out was next, which he said was written 4-3, because the second baseman was considered player four and he threw the ground ball to the first baseman, player three. The man at second had advanced to third on the play. Then a fielder's choice — FC on the scorecard — got the runner out at home. Jenna paid close attention: one on at first, two outs. The Dodger's catcher was up now. Then a wild pitch: WP. The runner scampered to second.

Her father grew agitated. Jenna held her breath. The crack of the bat on the ball startled her, the eerie way it sounded so long after the batter appeared to make contact.

"Holy shit! You can kiss that one goodbye." Joe put both hands over his eyes before collecting himself. "Well, Pork Chop. We're in one 'mell of a hess,' as my daddy used to say."

He rolled up one leg of his jeans, revealing a bulging tube sock, and removed a flask from the elastic band.

"Where's your mom with my Coke? Unbelievable." He paused. "Porks, listen. This thing with me and your mom. You know you can count on me, right?"

But Jenna's eyes were fixed on the game. She didn't like it when her dad drank anything besides beer. It made him selfish, like a bratty kid. She didn't think she could answer his question anyway. Jenna did not know if she could count on him; she thought probably not. Already she missed crawling into bed between her parents, feeling safe surrounded by their warm, yeasty smells. She usually only did it after a nightmare or if there was lightning. But knowing she couldn't wedge herself into their double bed if she wanted to made her sad. She had a feeling there were other things she would miss, too; things she hadn't even thought of yet.

"Mama loves you," she blurted out. At first, she thought Joe didn't hear her, but when she stole a look at him, he was waiting for her to go on.

"Did she say that?" He seemed surprised and pleased, leaning back and letting his knees fall open. "Ha. Interesting. What else?"

Jenna blushed.

"C'mon, Pork Chop. You can tell me." He grinned his charming lop-sided smile. Jenna's thoughts churned; she wanted desperately to retrieve something that would make him happy.

"She said that you were her asshole."

Her dad's eyebrows shot up. "That sounds about right," he said grimly, narrowing his eyes and swigging straight out of the flask.

Jenna face flushed and she felt a familiar aching in her throat that always preceded tears. She had said the wrong thing or hadn't said it right. The words didn't sound the same as when her mother had said them.

The Dodgers got another man on with a single to right, and he promptly stole second. She recognized Steve Garvey as he came to the plate and singled neatly to centerfield, sending the runner home.

Joe took another drink, scribbling furiously in the scorecard. "Jesus. Three to nothing!"

A ground out finished off the Dodgers and Jenna's mom was back, easing into their row with Boo on one hip and a cardboard tray with a brat and giant pretzel in her other hand. Boo had a Cardinals hat on top of his curls.

"What the hell?" Joe nodded at the cap. But his attention was back to the field as Lou Brock hit a lead-off single.

Jenna's mom shrugged. "Isn't he cute?" She took the brat and passed the pretzel to Jenna. "I thought you could share with Boo."

Jenna's throat tightened. She didn't like pretzels.

"Where's my cotton candy?" she asked in a small voice, although she knew the answer.

"Oh, Jenna. I knew I forgot something. Boo had to pee and when we got out of the bathroom, he saw the hats and then I got the food and . . ." Her mother made a dismissive gesture, as if to say "what can you do?"

Jenna blinked a couple of times and widened her eyes, trying to keep them from spilling over. Joe would yell at her and Boo for crying, even if it was over something they couldn't help, like a skinned knee.

"There he goes!" Her dad leaped up, nearly knocking the pretzel out of the box, waving his arm around like the third-base coach. There was no touching Lou. Safe. SB: Stolen base.

"Did you see that?" Joe wobbled slightly as he reached back to push down his seat. "Wait. What's going on, Porks?"

"The stupid cotton candy," her mom said. "I can't remember everything."

"How about anything? Like my goddamn Coke?"

Jenna's mom looked surprised. Then her jaw tightened. "Get your own goddamn Coke."

"I believe I goddamn will." Joe put his arm awkwardly around Jenna. "Don't cry. Jesus. I'll get your cotton candy in a while, okay?"

But Joe kept his eyes on the game, as if he wished he were on the field, not here where she was at all.

"How about that, Pork Chop? The Cardinals just scored."

The Cardinals tied it up in the fifth. An error by the Dodger third baseman had set up a two-run homer. Ted Simmons hadn't had much of a night so far, though. A ground out and a pop fly. Then he had hit into a double play. But Jenna felt the Cards might pull it out. It was a new ballgame now, her dad told her.

In the meantime, Joe had emptied his flask and all the contraband beers were gone.

"What's the matter?" Jenna's mom had finally asked, after the argument about the Coke and the inning of silence that followed. "This can't be about a stupid soda."

"What do you think is wrong, Doodle?" He didn't look at her.

"I don't know."

"I guess I'm just being an asshole then. Your asshole," he laughed a little too loudly, his mouth wide open, loose and wet. "But not for long."

Jenna's mom looked confused for a few seconds. Then she coolly remade her face and turned her gaze to Jenna, who squirmed. Her mom's face grew hard.

"Well, praise the fucking lord," she said, moving abruptly to the aisle seat. Boo was on her lap, then off; up the stairs and down. He crouched and made a pile of popcorn kernels and trash he found beneath the seats, his hands and face streaked with dirt. Jenna's mother didn't notice. She smoked cigarette after cigarette, perking up only to flirt with the greasy-haired beer man. She slowly crossed her long smooth legs as he poured a foamy Busch into a plastic cup.

"You want some of that?" Joe asked the beer man, nodding at Jenna's mom. "Go ahead. Help yourself."

"Screw you, Joe," her mother said. Jenna thought the beer man looked embarrassed.

"I'd like some," the toothless old man piped up. Joe ignored him.

"Let's go, Pork Chop." Her dad started to get up but couldn't on the first try. Then he unfolded himself from his seat and started down the aisle, Jenna trailing behind. "Excuse me," he said to her mom when they reached the end of the row, as though she were just some stranger.

"Take Boo. I've about had it with him. With this whole thing." Her mother pulled her knees to one side as they squeezed past without touching her.

"C'mon, Boo-Boo." He scooped the boy up and put him under his arm like a log. They reached the concourse and Joe set Boo on his feet, which were somehow missing their sandals.

"Potty!" Boo announced, grabbing his pants and holding himself.

"What?" Joe turned in a slow circle. He seemed dazed by the lights and the crowd that moved fluidly past them like a river closing around a sand bar. "Seriously, Boo?" He sighed. "Number one or number two?"

Boo's brow furrowed in concentration as he held up a starfish hand and carefully folded the pinky beneath his thumb. "Free."

"Free? What the hell is he saying, Pork Chop?"

Jenna was losing patience. Didn't her dad know anything?

"Three," Jenna said. Her father stared open-mouthed, uncomprehending, as if Jenna was speaking another language. "Number three. He needs to do both. Number one and number two."

"Jesus Christ. Okay." He grabbed Boo's hand. "Which way?"

Jenna pointed out the sign for the men's room where the concourse curved and seemed to disappear. Her dad squinted and shook his head.

"Alrighty then," he said, and started for the restroom. He turned back to look at Jenna, who hadn't moved. "I guess you better wait here."

She watched them shuffle off hand-in-hand, her father leaning slightly to one side because he couldn't stand straight or Boo was so short, she wasn't sure which. They vanished into a doorway and Jenna turned her attention to the hustle-bustle of the concourse. She smelled hamburgers and her stomach growled. She hadn't eaten since lunch, except for choking down a bite of pretzel. She wished her father had given her money. Boo would be forever in the bathroom with all he had to do in there. Maybe she could find the cotton candy and then lead her dad there when he finally got out with Boo.

Jenna looked around. She didn't think they had come in the way her dad had just gone. She remembered walking by the women's bathroom, which was the opposite way. Jenna walked slowly, trying to memorize where she was, where they had climbed the steps to reach the concourse. There was the popcorn vendor's red-and-gold cart. The beer stand. The hot dog man.

She rounded another bend and nearly ran into a giant cardinal holding a bat. Jenna had never seen such a big stuffed animal and wondered if it was someone in costume. But the bird — with its Cardinal hat and jersey — had freaky fake eyes instead of eyeholes and didn't flinch when she touched its beak. Behind the bird, the small souvenir store practically exploded with Cardinal shirts, pennants, baseballs and gloves. There were rows of hats like the one Boo got, too. But the baby cardinals by the entrance were what drew her in.

A fake tree stump held an oversized nest made from sticks and paper mâché that was filled with plush red, black-masked birds. A stylish woman and a girl with smooth blond hair in a red bow stood at the display. The girl pointed at first one, then another of the birds, her mother patiently lifting out each one in turn. Jenna edged up to the nest and reached for a bird, too.

She had never felt anything so soft. Jenna stroked the bird's red fur with the tip of one of her chewed nails, delighted at the line she made, a velvety path that could be easily smoothed away and retraced. The bird had a tiny white St. Louis Cardinal's t-shirt and fit perfectly in the palm of her hand. The eyes were not fake or crazy, but knowing. As if the bird understood her.

"I want this one, Mommy," the girl finally said. "And I want a megaphone, too."

Jenna waited for the mother to get angry with the girl for being so greedy. But to her amazement, the woman laughed. She reached for her daughter's hand and headed to the register. Jenna had forgotten about paying. The sticker on the cardinal's shirt said "$9.99."

Even if she asked her dad for the bird instead of cotton candy, it was too much.

She was just about to place the cardinal back in the nest when she saw the sign by the ball caps: $14.99. Jenna felt an odd twinge and her face began to burn. Before she could think, she had stretched up her shirt and tucked the cardinal inside the sweaty waistband of her shorts.

"Isn't that just the cutest little thing ever?"

Jenna eyes widened in alarm, but the lady behind the register was talking to the mother and daughter, placing their bird in a small, white-handled sack. Jenna turned her lumpy front away from the register. She could see the giant Cardinal outside the store. She took a breath and made her way outside, counting her steps to distract herself from thinking about getting caught. One, two, three. . . would someone tell her parents? Four, five, six… would she go to jail?

Seven.

Out on the concourse once more, Jenna released her breath, her heart pounding beneath her shirt. She moved quickly away from the souvenir store. She reached into her waistband and drew out the cardinal, damp and disheveled. Jenna couldn't believe he was hers, the giddy, sparkly feeling inside her overcoming the sick knowledge that she had stolen him.

Jenna rounded another bend and there it was: the cotton candy. She recognized the old man with the colorfully stained apron and shyly made her way up to the machine. He was hanging pillows of cotton candy in plastic bags on the silver poles attached to the cart.

"Ah, I see you are back." The man had a thick gray-black mustache that turned down around his mouth, making him look sad even when he smiled. "I think you forget about me, eh? I see you like the cotton candy, too." He patted the sizable stomach beneath his tight apron.

Jenna colored and nodded, stretching her shirt down self-consciously. The crowd inside the stadium cheered, and she wondered vaguely what she might have missed. And who was keeping the scorecard? Maybe she should find her dad and Boo.

"I show you how to make the cotton candy. You like pink. Am I right?"

The man laughed a throaty chuckle as he reached for a carton the size of a half-gallon of milk. He pulled a worn, three-legged stool toward the machine and sat. Then he poured a stream of neon pink sugar into the bowl and slid a paper cone off a nearby stack.

Jenna was mesmerized. Fuzzy puffs began to build around the bowl's perimeter before breaking off and blowing across the bottom like hot pink tumbleweeds. The man edged the cone around the bowl, twisting it so the wafting sugar attached in even tufts.

"Can I try?" she whispered, almost afraid to break the spell of the magical machine. The old man laughed, his mustache wiggling, and handed her a cone. Jenna reached for it, shifting the cardinal from her right hand to her left.

"Like this." The man stood close behind her and guided her sweaty hand with his. The sugar began to stick to the cone as they twisted it around, until it looked like a clown wig. It was perfect, a warm pink nest of spun sugar.

"There you are!" Jenna jumped at her mother's voice. She was marching toward them, a security guard on her heel, Joe with a hangdog look and Boo on his hip a few steps further behind. Jenna had never seen her mother so angry, her beautiful face red and contorted.

"What are you doing?" Jenna's mom was beside her and the cotton candy man, her breath coming out in hard puffs. She clutched Jenna's closest arm, her fingers encircling the plump bicep. Jenna panicked and dropped both the cotton candy and the stuffed bird into the bowl.

"My cardinal!"

Jenna's mother released her hold on Jenna, leaving a white bloodless handprint. Off balance, Jenna fell on her bottom, her polyester shorts clinging to the rough surface of the concrete floor, tearing a series of tiny runs in the seat. Her chest felt as if she'd swallowed a baseball. Then she was pulled off the ground and into the strong arms of the security guard.

"Are you okay?" His eyes were very blue. "Your parents were pretty worried."

Jenna nodded her head. But his kindness unloosened the hard lump in her chest and tears began to leak out of the corners of her eyes. "I . . . dropped my bird."

The cardinal sat ensnared in a web of pink sugar. The guard put Jenna down gently and reached into the machine, retrieving the bird with his thumb and forefinger.

"Where did you get that?" Jenna's mom looked suspicious. "You don't have any money." Then she looked daggers at the cotton candy man. "You sicko."

The security guard knelt down by Jenna. "Is this your bird, Jenna? Did you buy it?" His tone of voice suggested that he already knew the answer to the question.

"Did he give it to you?" Jenna's mom was in the cotton candy man's face, poking him in the chest with her index finger. "Is that how you lure kids in? Toys? Candy?"

The man held out his pink-and-blue-stained hands in confusion.

"Settle down, ma'am." The guard had stepped between Jenna's mom and the cotton candy man. A small, curious crowd had begun to form, sensing trouble or entertainment or both.

"Settle down? He had his hands and God knows what else on her and I . . ."

"Jenna?" The security guard's eyes were trying to hold hers and he had a slight frown. She scanned all the faces — the guard, her mom, the cotton candy man — all turned toward her, all wanting different answers. But she wasn't going to talk. She would just go to jail.

"It's hers. I bought it for her." Joe took a half step forward out of the crowd. Jenna had almost forgotten about him. He gave her a nod, as if they were on the same team.

"What?" This incensed Jenna's mom even further. "Oh, I get it. If I spend money, it's a stupid waste. If you spend it, you're Father of the Year."

"Doodle, listen." Joe tried to edge his way into the circle, Boo wide-eyed by his side. "This man found her, took care of her, for Christ's sake. We should be thanking him."

"What the hell do you know? You fucking lost her in the first place." She pleaded her case with the crowd. "He took her brother to the bathroom, left her outside and forgot her."

"All right. Everyone take a breath," the security guard said. "Let's be grownups."

Jenna's mom seemed subdued by his reprimand, crossing her arms over her chest and shifting her weight from one manicured, sandaled foot to the other. "I can't believe this," she muttered.

The crowd broke up. The show was over. Joe just shrugged. For his part, Boo was holding up one finger, pee running down his bare legs unchecked and soaking into Joe's jeans. Joe didn't even notice.

"I'm just going to take down some information before you all leave." The security guard pushed his hat further back onto his head and rubbed the bridge of his nose. "But you need to keep a better eye on your kiddos. This is the big city, you know?"

*　　　*　　　*

As soon as they were out of sight of the guard, Jenna's mom yanked her arm until Jenna thought it would pop from its socket. She was too surprised to cry.

"Don't you ever do that again," her mother bent down and whispered thickly. "Disappear and don't tell anyone where you're going. Just like your dad."

Back at their seats, her father shrank back into his seat, unable or unwilling to look at the rest of them. Jenna saw the trampled, beer-stained scorecard beneath his feet. She paused at the end of the row with her sticky red bird, unsure what to do next. Her mother stood stiffly beside her, holding a soggy, sleeping Boo against her chest. Organ music swelled from the stands below and the crowd answered back: Da-da-da-da-ta-da… Charge!

Her mom and Boo were leaving. She had called Aunt Mena from a pay phone on their way back to the seats and she would be arriving outside any minute. Jenna could either come along or stay. "I don't really give a damn," her mother said.

Jenna looked down at the ruined bird, its red plush gummy with sugar that had blackened from the grime on her hands. She looked at her disheveled, pee-stained father, who — over the course of the evening — had become everything he hated in everyone else: Ordinary. A forgetter. A mistake.

"Pork Chop? We're going to extra innings."

Jenna could not have told anyone why. But in that hot, sticky moment in July, 1978, with the stadium lights buzzing and her mother's foot tapping impatiently, she decided to stay. Maybe it was the way the little cardinal looked at her with its reproachful eyes (she would end up cramming the bird in the crack of the folded, empty seat beside her and leaving it). But later — much later — Jenna will think that perhaps her decision had more to do with the hopefulness of those extra innings, when the score was tied and anything was possible. A whole new ballgame. Of course, she could not have known how it would turn out: the Dodgers taking a one-run lead in the top of the fifteenth and the Cardinals with a chance to win it with one on, two out, and Ted Simmons swaggering to the plate.

What Jenna will remember is standing beside her dad. And how the remaining crowd — the diehards, those who had stayed on as the clock inched toward midnight — stood, too, clapping and cheering Simba on, going wild as he brought back his bat and swung like a king. How there was the sharp crack of the bat and the collective intake of breath as the ball went up, up, up until Jenna lost it in the lights. Then after what felt like minutes or hours or days, the center fielder's glove closed with an efficient snap and the long, grueling game was finally over.

The Crossing

Jenny Crews

Lois had cancer in one of her legs.
She tilted when she walked.
She said the pain wasn't too much to gripe about.
On white winter days it slowed her up a bit.
Lois didn't like the snow.
She liked Africa. She craved hot, windy jeep rides
in the jungle, her leg propped up with a brown leather strap
to hold it steady, to make her look like a tough old gal.
She read hardback books about Africa when she ate,
hefty nonfiction works, far bigger than her meals.
Lois liked eating Kraft Macaroni and Cheese.
She liked Coca-Cola, and raisins.
If she'd lived in Africa, she would have been a forager,
a berry picker. Yes, she would be Lois, Nairobi Princess,
stepping outside and smelling yellow fruits,
knowing just where to find them, just how to eat them,
seeds and skin.
She would know where to walk in Kenya.
But not here. Not in this frigid hemisphere.
Here, Lois, while crossing a street against a quick yellow light
one March, was hit too hard by a Buick.
There was color in her death, a red not so real to her
as the rest of us might see.
Lois, Bus Rider of #3 Elm Street,
in the city of Springfield-proper,
wedged beneath the front
bumper of a bright blue car,
had finally found her place
in this twisted scheme of ordinary things.
Here was the passage to holy Africa.

At the Table

Jenny Crews

—on the eve of the 2020 election

They shut ole Trudy down, Mom said
over 40 years ago.
Trudy had been Mom's fortune teller,
Mom's one to tell the truth about, and to.
They closed up her practice
since she was doing readings
over a dead chicken,
Mom explained to me as we were drinking tea
when I was in my 20s.
The health department in Joplin, it had been,
that shut old Trudy down.
Did she use the same white chicken?
I wondered, and still do.
Flies collecting on flesh, over and over. Again.
It never hit me until a few years back—
Trudy probably slit that poor fowl's
throat so she could glean a glimpse of future.
Women paid good money, in the 60s,
to sit beside the blood of something other than a lamb—
to watch an elder woman who must have smelled
of purple talc and liniment, speak above the dead.
She—this trusted one—would convince,
reveal to them what they wished
they might find easier to tell themselves.
All is as it should be.
Your children will be all. Right.

Vinyl

Jenny Crews

Watch out for a woman with a white vinyl bag
on her arm if she also wears white vinyl shoes—
pumps with two- or three-inch heels, plastic
torn and dented. She wears red lipstick, but
not that of a cool blue tint. No, she wears red
in shades of yellow, though her skin calls out
for something far less warm. She sports short jean
skirts with wide belts, vinyl and brown in color.
She wears, most often, a silver-toned cross,
either hung from a bracelet or a neck chain
cut only just too tight, Ozark-bound.
Her hair smells of *Aqua Net* or *White Rain*,
pungent, stale and bitter.
Watch out for this woman with the white vinyl bag
because, when she decides to crack it open,
spill the contents on your kitchen table after an evening
beside you in your backroom bed,
you'll be witness to all that's inside her—
not just inside her purse.
Pepper spray that's a few years old,
tampons with wrappers torn from them
like peels from bananas,
breath mints, loose from foil, covered
in matted hair and lint.
You'll find, scattered in the pitch,
wadded tissues, half-used,
open boxes of old raisins, once gold—
now purple with color from uncapped
lip pencils, eye liners, mascara.
There will be, in the mix, an old leather
coin purse, pieced together from remnants
on a warehouse floor.

The purse will hold nickels, dimes,
but no copper pennies. No quarters for this
woman with one white vinyl bag, vinyl shoes—
this woman who, last night, begged
you to call your house her home.

Who is Loyal?

Lynn Morrow

Clarity about who was loyal or not during the Civil War in the Ozarks is a dominant theme in military records. Officers held formal interviews in the local office of the provost marshal. Of course, non-combatants in civilian clothes took great interest in what evidence was presented by either side of the allegations. Some residents took a stance of neutrality much to the chagrin of the more Radical Unionists late in the war. The provost interviews were commonplace and resembled a modern administrative hearing in state government. Which civilians (Union or Rebel sympathizers) sold supplies to mounted militia units on scout in the countryside was often an irritation to the "other side." Disputes could involve military and civilian courts.

In March 1864, a *cause celeb* in Rolla erupted over one of the most public places in town, the King Hotel. Union officers regularly patronized the boarding house on Rolla Street, east of the courthouse. In early 1861, carpenter Richard Wade built the two-story, frame building for slaveholder and storekeeper, Solomon King. Wade was "an unconditional Union man," and in spring 1861 when local leaders chanted for Southern supremacy prior to the arrival of the Union army on the railroad, "had to leave Rolla without getting a settlement from Solomon King." Richard Wade later returned to his Spring Creek Township farm, living near Edgar Springs, but he also accepted carpentry projects in Rolla. In the face of earlier citizen grumblings about King, military authorities required a $3,000 bond of hotelier King in October 1862.

But, in March 1864, Richard Wade, James Bradford, George Bezoni, and twenty-six others drew up a petition charging Solomon King with disloyalty. They included details that King still owed "eight or nine hundred dollars" to Wade, and submitted their evidence to provost marshal Capt. Isaac Gray. Gray's report to his superiors said King was "strongly suspected of being an accessory" to the death of Wade's brother, Robert, in Spring Creek Valley. Capt. Gray told Mayor D. R. Parsons that he took steps to have King's property confiscated, then wrote to Col. Albert Sigel on March 28th that he would soon forward "more evidence that King harbored bushwhackers since he took the oath of allegiance." One wonders during the time, if while Wade worked in Rolla, refugees James Bradford and George Bezoni, who shared Wade's Radical politics, encouraged the affidavit.[1]

James Bradford told Capt. Gray that he had known King, a long-time Spring Creek resident, for thirty-five years. In spring 1861, related Bradford, King came to his house near Licking and "I went with him to Houston, Texas County, he told me on the way that Gov. [Claiborne] Jackson had sent to St. Louis to purchase eighteen thousand dollars' worth of powder," and suggested they would find a use for it locally. Bradford continued: "I know Mr. King's general character well, since the war [I] know him to be a notorious Rebel, have often heard him abuse Federal soldiers. . . . He had six sons in the Rebel army, and one step son, who was killed in the brush."

Petitioner Richard W. Wade, who had lived in the neighborhood since 1854 and had held the road overseer office, echoed James Bradford's accusations. He claimed that in May 1861—almost three years earlier—King took "two six mule teams of government wagons" to his house. Later, King loaded these wagons with kegs of powder, but disguised them as bacon to take to Wood Rodgers on Big Piney River at the Nathaniel K. Rodgers' steam mill, where they would distribute the powder to rebels throughout Texas and Phelps Counties. Then, King went to Houston where he made speeches that "induced a great many men to join the Rebel army." Wade claimed he saw King "harboring Rebels and Bushwhackers frequently at his house" on Spring Creek into summer of 1862. By then, Col. Robert Wooding Rodgers was with the Confederacy in Texas. The memoir of Ai Edgar Asbury wrote that Rodgers, and young attorneys in Houston, W. H. H. Thomas and himself, transported three wagons of powder from Jefferson City to Houston for State Guard use in the Civil War.[2]

Terrill Hefflin piled on to the King attack. Hefflin arrived in Rolla in spring 1863 and settled three miles from town. King, who was managing his hotel at the time, sold "two cows and a pony" to Hefflin, who paid King in Confederate money that he had acquired in an Arkansas stock trade. Terrill said that King charged "Union soldiers two bits a piece for meals, but charged me nothing, believing me to be one of his stripe." Lastly, Hefflin proclaimed King "to be a deep died Rebel."

The provost marshal acted – he seized King's hotel and turned it over to Wade. Although nothing was legally settled in spring 1864, gossip in Rolla fueled the rumors about King's nefarious powder trip to Big Piney River. Many in Rolla knew that King was one of the first to publicly declare an oath of allegiance to the Union which was printed in a June 1861 newspaper and that locals elected him the same month to serve as a town councilman. The clamor over the hotel may have encouraged the provost marshal's office to call in citizens to tell what else they knew about suspicious people in their midst. By May 1864, accusatory affidavits by more than a dozen men were being signed in the presence of the provost marshal housed in the court-house. The commanding officer allowed Wade and militia Lt. Col. and merchant, Homer F. Fellows, to also take possession of King's four town lots west of the courthouse. Militarily, Rolla was peaceful during spring-summer 1864. But, in this very public dispute, Capt. Gray failed in his quest to obtain government possession of King's property to allow Richard Wade to occupy it very long. The King investigation must have provided entertainment for many even though a visiting circus performed that summer in Rolla.

Just prior to an assembly of witnesses to interview about the loyalty of those around Rolla and Phelps County, Elijah Perry, a prominent attorney, justice-of-the-peace, election judge, Union officer, president of the Board of Assessors, and wartime state representative from Phelps County wrote to his superior in St. Louis, Col. J. P. Sanderson, provost marshal general. On April 22, 1864, Perry submitted a list of seventy-one men who represented the "leading and influential men of the County of Phelps . . . men of standing and character." The list included their occupations and "political views and P.O. addresses." There was but one "rebel sympathizer" listed in Rolla, lawyer Samuel Williams, then, grist miller Phillip Jackson on Little Piney Creek, and a half-dozen men at St. James.[3]

Perry's sixty-three Unionists embodied the heart of the Rolla-area private sector economy and professional class. Among them were

George Benzoni, E. W. Bishop, Joseph Campbell & Patrick Long, Robert Case, J. A. Dillon, Robert P. Faulkner, H. W. Fellows, C. H. Frost, Warren H. Graves, G. Grayson, William James (of Maramec Iron Works), Solomon King, D. R. Parsons, W. G. Pomeroy, C. P. Walker, Isaac Warmoth, Benj. Wishon, W. C. York, and more. Was York's current business partner, the wealthy James A. Bates, left off Perry's list because York had political standing, reputation as a Rolla town founder, and that as a merchant "everyone knew" that he was an ally of merchant Bates? Perhaps. Or, maybe everyone considered Bates a visiting refugee and that his permanent residence lay in Texas County. The obvious irony of course was that the affidavits from Rolla denizens in the Solomon King provost case accused several of Elijah Perry's Unionists as southern sympathizers, begging the ongoing question, who is loyal? Three days later, Wade filed a complaint in justice-of-the-peace court against Phillip Jackson, one of the admitted "rebel sympathizers" on Perry's list for stealing his shotgun, powder, shot pouch, and spurs, a case that continued into the fall.

Meanwhile, in spring 1864, residents gave conflicting testimony to the provost marshal that cast serious shadows on Solomon King, James A. Bates, Lindsey L. Coppedge, Isaac Bradford, and several men with inconsistent reputations on both the Union and Confederate sides of the loyalty issue. Settling scores, by whatever means, runs through Civil War histories. But rather than violence, attacks on one's character and damming accusations that led to financial losses, may be more common than physical assaults. As provost marshal appointments revolved in Rolla, newly arrived officers continued investigations, or launched their own, of allegations identifying "rebel sympathizers." Furthermore, the army wanted to know who among those who had already supplied goods and services to the army should "not receive pay for forage and materials furnished to the Government" because of their southern sympathies. It grated on some Unionists' sentiments of loyalty when they saw "sympathizer families" come to Rolla and present a voucher to the provost marshal for cash reimbursement of supplies given to a Union militia on scout. Reputations and money were on the line.

The event that triggered the initial inquisition was Robert W. Wade's killing near Lindsey Coppedge's Mill on February 1, 1864. Stone mason Wade had earlier lived near builder Andrew Malcolm in Rolla and likely worked on the new courthouse. Rolla's Radical Unionists looked to place blame for his homicide. New provost marshal, Capt. Thomas B. Reed, and his assistant, J. C. McCain, conducted interviews in May 1864. The individual sessions concluded with a section in their report about "suspected southern sympathizers." Another list specifically identified who "in your opinion should not receive pay." The interrogatories enumerated estimates on the economic worth, land holdings, and family circumstances of distrustful persons. The provost examination of Phelps County property assessments available in the courthouse revealed a pattern of accusations against the same names. Several names not on the "rebel sympathizer" list do show up in the "should not receive pay" category. No explanation for this inconsistency is in the report.

Mechanic Robert M. Peck characterized rebel sympathizer Solomon King owning "about 1,000 acres of land worth $4.00 per acre, house & lot in Rolla on which he resides is worth $4,000." Peck said he didn't know the worth of his horses, cattle, and household furniture. On another suspect, L. L. Coppedge "owns a water mill and some land and personal property worth some $10,000. He has a family. Isaac Bradford in Relfe Township has land said to be worth $8,000. Moses Bradford [then in a Confederate prison] resides in same neighborhood and has land and is said to be worth $5,000. He has a family." Those whom Peck identified as unworthy to receive government pay were Solomon King, Tyree Lingo (who had about 1,500 acres in Roubidoux Township, Texas County), Samuel Williams (lawyer in Rolla who represented southerners in court and contracted as a Phelps County government attorney), merchant and Rolla developer John Webber, Dr. John Hyer (paroled Confederate, then residing in Rolla, managing a drug store near James A. Bates's residence, and required to report daily to the provost marshal), and F. M. Wishon (Lindsey Coppedge's son-in-law), who commonly clerked in the Coppedge store on Spring Creek.

The accuser, contractor Richard W. Wade, who had performed recent repairs on the new courthouse where the interviews took place, grieved for his slain brother and was determined to battle the authorities over the future ownership of the King Hotel. Wade accused twenty-two men, primarily residents on Spring Creek and Little Piney Creek, who were complicit or had knowledge of the crime. "L. L. Coppedge [now living in Dillon with the Wishons] with about 500 acres of land well improved, think it is $10.00 per acre, he has a water mill & carding machine, considerable personal property, a wife and 7 children, one married; F. M. Wishon, resides with Coppedge, near Dillon, has considerable property, he has a family; Issac Bradford resides ½ mile from Coppedge's Mill on Spring Creek has about 600 acres land well improved worth $10.00 per acre, has personal property, wife and 4 children and 2 sons in Rebel army; also has a large farm in Texas County" [where he operated Stephen Taylor's steam saw mill near Licking to provide plank to the Union army]; and "Solomon King resides 3 miles from Coppedge's Mill on Spring Creek, has 500 acres land well improved worth $10.00 per acre [Robert Peck's interview said 1,000 acres worth $4.00 per acre], some personal property, wife and 2 children with him, 6 sons in Rebel army, lately moved to Rolla, town property in Rolla worth $3,000."

The twenty-two men identified represented a group of well-heeled agriculturalists and millers who occupied the rich farm lands of Spring and Little Piney Creeks and the prairie uplands around Edgar Springs. Most owned acreages from 300 to 600 acres, and included William Arthur, Dr. Robert B. Cowan, Thomas Dennison, John Jackson, John Loftin, Jackson Nichols, Allen Stephens, Lewis Wright, and others. Richard Wade was unequivocal when he concluded, "All of the above named should not receive pay." Here and elsewhere those who were accused of disloyalty were public men of business and social position; Coppedge, King, and Wishon had all served as election judges for Relfe Township.

George A. Bezoni was even more emphatic in his accusations. Bezoni was a New York Italian, who with his wife and eight children had immigrated to Roubidoux Township in Texas County just before the war and described himself to the census taker as a farmer. Bezoni's son-in-law, a painter, came, too; George's brother, John, joined them later. The brothers joined Kansas abolitionist turned Union Lt. Col. S. N. Wood for an enlistment in cavalry duty at the Houston post. After returning home as civilians, in summer 1862, Col. William Coleman's irregulars led by the Darden brothers, former Rolla merchants, called at Bezoni's and stole his horse, household effects, and rummaged around until they found and appropriated his hidden guns. The Bezoni family "refugeed" to Rolla and made a formal claim to the army for their loss of $183 in property [$4,816]. By May 1863, the enterprising Bezoni was a Rolla election judge at the county courthouse; he contracted with the county court to bury a pauper; then, he bought two town lots in August 1863, and managed a small store. Bezoni was acting city marshal in May 1864 and soon became the actual town marshal. He assailed the reputations of men of his brief acquaintance who had kinfolk who sided with the Confederacy, or rumored to have. He went on to allege their duplicity in a personal report to the provost marshal.[4]

Like Richard Wade, newcomer Bezoni identified prominent Rolla and countryside dwellers for disloyalty. He started with Tyree Lingo, who "had considerable real estate in Texas County, think it is in the hands of the United States, if not it should be, has a wife & 6 children, were in good circumstances." Lingo in fact had three farms, his home place of 630 acres, and tenants on two others that totaled another 774 acres. Bezoni had cause to be disgusted by Lingo. A lawyer and farmer, Lingo became a "secession orator" in spring 1861 and helped raise the "rattle snake flag" on the Houston town square. However, in a change of heart, Lingo guided Lt. Col. Eppstein's militia scout south in July 1862 and suffered the crippling of his horse for which Col. Albert Sigel requested an indemnity for Lingo's damages.

In October 1862, Lt. Joseph Reed, provost marshal at Waynesville, complained about the "wealthy and influential" Lingo. Although under bond, alleged Reed, Lingo discouraged Union enlistments and "endeavored to frighten men to go South . . . and conducts villainous schemes [on them] that it is useless to arrest these ignoramuses who are only the dupes of designing scoundrels." Later in the month, Reed ordered Lingo's family out of his federal lines to Rolla. He wrote Col.

John Glover that the "female members of the family have at all times the utmost bitterness against the Federal Government and Federal officers and soldiers." In Rolla, Lingo, who had been permitted to sign the official roll of attorneys to practice law in Phelps County, did not shy from the public spotlight, and earned modest income as an attorney for clients at the courthouse. On December 17, 1862, Lingo signed an oath to become a Phelps County election judge and immediately solicited Gov. Hamilton Gamble for a commission as a notary public in Rolla.

Union citizens grumbled to the military about Lingo. In August 1863, Capt. S. R. Squires reported to Gen. Thomas Davies that Lingo was a horse thief and was connected with a stagecoach mail robbery. By October, Maj. O. P. Newberry requested of Gen. Davies a sergeant and ten men to go arrest Lingo "as I am satisfied that a prompt movement will expose a long series of crimes." Davies asked why not five men and Newberry reported that "five men cannot watch all the parties implicated in this matter." On October 18th, Newberry had Lingo in the Ft. Wyman prison where he was later transferred to Gratiot Street Prison, St. Louis.

Authorities in St. Louis prepared to try Lingo before a military commission. In January 1864, officers concluded that the expense of paying for so many witnesses to come by train to the trial was too much, so they decided to send Lingo to Capt. Issac Gray, provost marshal in Rolla, to appear for his military trial. Lingo, to pay for his defense, deeded 120 acres northeast of Plato to W. G. Pomeroy to retain legal services. Accused, in part, of horse stealing, witnesses reported that Lingo had turned over a horse to Capt. E. B. Grimes in Rolla. In January 1864, the military commission in Rolla placed Lingo under a steep $5,000 bond, securities guaranteed by James A. Bates, J. B. Vance, and Aaron Von Wormer (later, the bond was transferred to Lingo's neighbors living in Roubidoux Township, Texas County). Lingo's parole required that he remain in Rolla unless the provost marshal granted permission to travel. The embattled Lingo resumed attorney work for clients in civilian court. In the end, C. P. Walker, editor and printer for government work, considered Lingo as one of "the biggest Union toads in the puddle," since Lingo recently "learned to love the constitution." Walker claimed that Lingo had permanently reformed his position on the Union, a statement that complainant Richard Wade did not accept. Lingo appeared before a judge advocate at a military commission in May 1864, but was not convicted of wrongdoing.[5]

The New Yorker Bezoni continued his appraisal: "Solomon King has a large farm on Spring Creek, also house & lots in Rolla worth about $18,000, farms, etc.; Dr. John Hyer resides in Rolla, has a large farm on Spring Lake [Lake Spring], also a small drug store in Rolla, he is worth about $10,000, has a family in good circumstance; James Addison Bates resides in Rolla, he has town lots & houses and is a partner of Judge William York in goods business, he has a number of farms & steam mills in Texas County, some personal property, he is worth $40,000, has a family in good circumstances; Judge William York resides in Rolla, has a farm 12 miles from Rolla on Springfield Road well improved worth about $5,000, also a portion of Bates in goods business in Rolla worth in all $12,000, family in good circumstance; R. J. McElhaney resides at Springfield, he is a partner of Jaccard & Co., extensive merchants in Springfield & Rolla, has a family in good circumstances, he is worth about $20,000; Warren H. Graves resides in Rolla, has considerable property in Rolla & Springfield, he is partner of Faulkner in the goods business, quite extensive, he is worth about $25,000. I do not know that he has a family." Bezoni didn't know much about Graves either, as he was a Republican newspaper publisher and wealthy land agent in Springfield, who lived part time in Rolla. Bezoni ended his accusations with lawyer Samuel Williams, and the merchant James A. McDonald on Roubidoux Creek, father of Pulaski County clerk, W. W. McDonald.[6]

Bezoni's wealth evaluations were close to the local government tax assessments that the Union army had secured at the courthouse. James A. Bates' 1860 valuations before he moved to Rolla, totaled over $48,000 [$1,403,322] as the wealthiest man in Texas County. In addition to these twelve rebel sympathizers, Bezoni further listed sixteen men who should not receive pay. His "no pay" additions included Lindsey Coppedge and Col. Henry F. Ormsby, country merchants who had provided Union militias with feed for horses and rest for men at their mill sites.

Onlookers must have rolled their eyes at Bezoni's inclusion of William C. York and Robert McElhaney, pillars of Unionism. But what Bezoni saw was that York and McElhaney were merchants who did business with people like James A. Bates. Bezoni was well aware of Bates' kith and kin connections among the Southern sympathizing families and that Bates had signed security bonds for several of them, including one of his sons who had a short stint with the rebels. The New Yorker took the position that Bates' role of straddling the middle ground of business reliability for Union efforts, but refused to emphatically deny any assistance to southern families, made Bates and those who befriended him all unworthy to participate in commercial profits. Bates and his friends were "guilty" by reason of association.

James Bradford, whom Col. Coleman's guerrilla band had earlier victimized in Texas County, came forward. He listed fifteen men who had a wide variety of wealth evaluations, but the group was not nearly as affluent as the Spring Creek men; Bradford's targets lived within a few miles of Licking. He included Joel Sherrill, "about 900 acres land well improved worth $4.00 per acre, some personal property, wife & two children in good circumstances; Spencer Mitchell, Sr., large well improved farm worth $2,500, personal property & wife; Thos. Dennison in Phelps County on the Batesville & Jeff City Road 25 miles from Rolla [on upper Spring Creek] has well improved farm worth $2,000, some personal property, has a wife & 5 children;" and concluded with Moses Freeman, Spencer Mitchell, Jr., William Thornton, and others. He judged the Sherrills, Mitchells, Dennisons, and Thompson Reed unworthy to receive pay for supplies already purchased by Union militias.

Capt. Reed's summary to Brig. Gen. Odon Guitar preserved Capt. William Monks' comments. His statement, however, was primarily about Howell County where Monks lived and seven Unionists who were killed there, 1861-62. He named ten men who shouldn't receive pay for forage given to the Union militias. Monks did confirm four "traitors" on James Bradford's list – Joel Sherrill, John Nichols, Thos. Dennison, and Spencer Mitchell. Judging from the documents available, it appears that no clear evidence could be marshaled in the accusations of the Radicals. Of interest is that Daniel Chamberlin, artist [photographer], also pointed to several public men who should not receive pay. They included Solomon King, Robert Case, John Webber, Samuel Williams, and Irishman Patrick Long of the firm of "Campbell & Long" in the dry goods business. It is obvious that a common thread in the listing of disloyal, affluent persons included those actively merchandising to the public and to the military. The identity of these commercial men suggests that brisk competition existed for the "government work," contracts and permits, and that the army tried to spread out the economic opportunities among those who had resources and networks to offer. The army depended upon reliable citizen vendors, especially those in sawmilling commerce who could deliver logs and plank, several of whom had relatives in the Confederacy.

In late March 1864, the provost marshal initiated steps to confiscate King's hotel and to allow Wade to occupy it. Solomon commenced a legal complaint over the injustice of losing it. The Wade-King conflict illustrates that their differences were about more than loyalty. King turned to attorney and Unionist Elijah Perry for representation.

Court depositions reveal that Wade and King had long-simmering differences. King had a well-developed farm in Spring Creek Valley and he managed a country store. Wade approached him for assistance. First, he signed a promissory note for $61.00 [$1,851] to King on March 8, 1858. A year and a half later, in August 1859, he opened an account at King's store. Wade purchased domestic items including cloth and thread, shoes and boots, matches and candles, tea and coffee, tobacco and salt, and paper. Bacon, beef, corn, oats, and lard were added to the meet the needs of his family and animals. Wade was still developing his farm and business, thus, King supplied nails, chalk lines, chisels, files, horseshoes, and scythes, and also hauled commodities for Wade in his wagon. Occasionally, Wade paid cash to King's hired hands. By then, Wade's purchases reached beyond $500 [$14,618], but King received only partial payments.

Meanwhile, on April 10, 1860, King and Wade signed a contract for Wade to construct a 25 feet x 50 feet barn with 16 feet walls for $200 [$5,847]; that contract was subsequently lost or destroyed. Before Wade had completely finished the barn, King hired him to build a hotel in Rolla that Wade began in May 1860. The hotel building was to be 20 feet x 40 feet. By August 1860, Wade had the building lot prepared and was waiting for King to haul timbers for the sleepers that would support the floor. King delayed, as he was busy with other preoccupations. Wade "kept urging him to be ready to haul to Rolla as I wanted to finish the job as I would be at home during the winter." King "put me off," said Wade, until January 1861.

Wade and his hands stayed in Rolla during winter to build the hotel. The construction project added an ell on the rear for a dining room. They built it of rough lumber, "not a plane to be put on it," as King wanted to finish and paint it himself. Wade and his hands completed the job in late April 1861, but too late for Wade to plant two of his own spring crops. Moreover, complained Wade to the court, his wife and children had to do all the winter work. Being much put upon, Wade wanted damages for their labor. Wade returned home in early May wanting to break more "new ground" for his agricultural improvements. King loaned two yoke of oxen for the work, but retrieved them before Wade had accomplished all the plowing in his fields. Before any further settlement between the two men took place, the Civil War began. Due to the presence of Southern anti-unionists in Rolla, Wade fled the area temporarily. Three years later, Wade brought his accusations of disloyalty and unpaid debts against King, and the hotelier countered with his own suit against Wade.[7]

Plaintiff King's case went to the Phelps County circuit court. There Judge Van Wormer negotiated with the litigants for arbitration and the court appointed three referees: E. W. Bishop, Andrew Malcolm, and C. H. Frost on March 26, 1864. The Rolla businessmen interviewed witnesses, several of whom were hands who had worked for Wade. They had to take into account Wade's unsatisfied note to King and his balance at King's store. The referees rejected Wade's damages claim for his family's work in the winter and crops lost in the field, as Wade had no special contract for the hotel and "could have quit at any time or refused to do the work." Wade did have legitimate charges for work on the hotel. He provided the lumber for the two-story building, its front portico, front door with side lights, windows, blinds, interior stairway, cellar door, and more. The court rendered its judgment on May 26, 1864. The arbitrators concluded on April 8, 1864, that Wade owed $52.39 to King and that the litigants split the court costs. Wade's denunciations against King to the military quickly faded.

Lastly, the difficulty that faced the beleaguered provost marshal office was illustrated by C. P. Walker's interview. Maj. Walker of the local Enrolled Missouri Militia (EMM), clerk of the county and circuit court, member of the defunct Board of Assessors for Phelps and Adjoining Counties, and publisher and founder of the local *Rolla Express* in July 1860 stated, "I do not know of any sympathizers to my personal knowledge." No one would have known the local population any better than Walker, and in view of his service on the Board of Assessors that had met weekly at the courthouse, his answer was an outright lie. Walker did name five men, "Union citizens killed by bushwhackers," two in Phelps County and three in Maries County. Walker's response to whom should not receive pay for "forage and materials furnished the Gov't" is an astonishing statement: "I know of no one furnishing forage to Gov't." This last response was apparently given by the moderate Unionist Walker so that he could "wash his hands" of any involvement in finger-pointing at local residents, even by reputation. The evasiveness of lukewarm Unionists demonstrates the extreme difficulty of a provost marshal residing at Rolla to identify, let alone eradicate, disloyalty.[8]

In June 1864, provost marshal Capt. Thomas Reed reported the results of Maj. C. P. Walker's interview and thirteen others to Brig. Gen. Odon Guitar. Reed understatedly presented his frustration in his second sentence, "C. P. Walker can furnish the names of no Rebel Sympathizers." Reed wrote that William Monks and George Bezoni "are now and have always been thoroughly Union. They are two of the best men in the State of Missouri. Not one of the other twelve witnesses classes them as Rebel Sympathizers and yet in all probability every one of the witnesses knows McElhaney and Graves as well if not better than Bezoni does." A dutiful Capt. Reed avoided making value judgements as to the veracity of those identified as disloyal, but reported what he heard and left any decision-making up to his superior, Gen. Guitar.

Guitar read the report and wrote his superior, Maj. Gen. Rosecrans, commander of the Department of Missouri in St. Louis. First, Guitar said that the petition process preceded his assignment to command the District of Rolla. Guitar's personal reaction was disgust at the answers of the petitioners. "In my opinion, the patriotism and self-sacrificing devotion of all the petitioners combined will never induce one of them to put his precious carcass in the way of a rebel bullet, their aspersions to the contrary notwithstanding." Rosecrans agreed. On June 23, 1864, Guitar received a response from St. Louis that authorized him "to convene a military commission for the trial of the petitioners, as in his opinion, have made false and malicious representations." The door to prosecute perjury was open. Back in Rolla, Gen. Guitar and his staff decided they had more productive work to do in the Ozarks. There is no record of any trial. Interrogation of civilians ceased and Gen. Guitar left Rolla in August. The incoming Rolla command also chose other work to do.

But, the dogged R. W. Wade did not remain quiet. He leveled more charges, this time against Phillip Jackson in civilian court. The defendant appealed to Mayor Daniel Parson's municipal court, where Jackson claimed that Phelps County inhabitants were prejudiced against him. Jackson's motion for a change of venue to Crawford County was approved, and Marshal George Bezoni shuffled the requisite paperwork. The case, which relied on witnesses from August 1861, was on Crawford County's docket for October 1864. But, before the court convened, Wade filed an additional case against Philip Jackson and his comrades in Rolla on September 6, 1864, one that added to his earlier charge that Jackson had stolen property at his house. Wade was not satisfied that the army in Rolla had not initiated any actions against his targeted Southern sympathizers.

The events described by Wade took place three years earlier on the same August 14, 1861, date he claimed Jackson stole his shotgun. Wade alleged that Jackson, John Edgar, and Jackson Nichols, "being armed with guns and pistols in a threatening way," assaulted him in his house near Edgar Prairie. They "seized and forced him" to accompany them on the public road and through the woods to Salem where they imprisoned him. Wade said that he spent one week in open air "exposed to the heat of the sun" and had to sleep on "the bare ground without anything to protect him from the chilling dews of the night;" his captors allowed him only "scraps of bread and refuse meat" to eat.[9]

Wade's tormentors then took him to Licking for a day suffering "twenty four hours without food." The following day, the group traveled to the Big Piney River "through the rain and mud, wading creeks in Texas County" and "compelled him to sleep at night on the bare ground in the mud and water." On the subsequent day, they traveled seven miles down Big Piney" and "for three days kept him in a certain log pen, without any covering to shelter him from the extreme heat of the sun, or from the rain or from the unhealthy dews of the night." According to popular wisdom the dews and fogs were the source of malaria and fevers.

The plaintiff's attorney concluded that Wade's false imprisonment lasted twelve days from August 14-26, 1861. Wade asked for $5,000 in damages as he was not only "greatly hurt, bruised, exposed and injured in health and endangered in life," but was also greatly exposed and injured in his credit and business. Elijah Perry notarized his statement for the court. The defendants, after several motions in Phelps County court over the next year, did receive a change of venue to Crawford County. After the war, in October 1866, the Crawford County court refused to hear the case and sent it back to Phelps County. There lawyers and the court issued subpoenas for the November 1866 term. The case file does not appear in the extant records suggesting that, once again, a festering dispute withered and died as time drained personal energy and financing.

Complaints related to the Civil War, like Richard Wade's, continued in high numbers until the 1880s. Plaintiffs in post-war Missouri sought financial relief hundreds of times for wartime personal and property insults, usually to no avail. Accusers and defenders occasionally argued in the streets of the Ozarks, sometimes with their fists, into the twentieth century.

Bibliography

[1] The investigation initiated by Richard Wade is in Union Provost Marshal Papers, March 18, 24, and 26, 1864, F1151, Missouri State Archives (hereinafter MSA), and March 1864 in F1610 and F1614, Union Provost Marshal Papers, Two or More Civilians, MSA. This essay is modified from "Bates and Lenox," a typescript in the State Historical Society of Missouri-Rolla, R1000 Lynn Morrow Papers.

[2] See *My Experience in the War 1861 to 1865 or A Little Autobiography by Ai Edgar Asbury*, Berkowitz and Compnay, 1894, SHS-Columbia. Asbury was the 1860 Texas County school commissioner and attended the May 1861 state convention in Jefferson City where he consulted with C. F. Jackson about the powder.

[3] "Leading and influential men" are in an April 22, 1864, Perry letter to Col. Sanderson, Union Provost Marshal Papers, Two or More Civilians, F1612, f. 703, MSA.

[4] Capt. Stephen H. Darden died on August 13, 1862, while Samuel B. survived, and after the war, returned to Rolla to work and live. The third and youngest brother, James R. Darden was also a local carpenter, but later moved to Kansas. The dollar amounts in brackets are from an inflation calculator and inserted only in selected places for the reader to imagine modern valuations.

[5] Lingo's $5,000 bond is listed on Mar. 31, 1864, Roll of Prisoners Received, Union Provost Marshal Papers, Two or More Civilians, F1610, f. 633, MSA.

[6] Bezoni's and others' statements are in Union Provost Marshal Papers, Two or More Civilians, May 1864, F1614, MSA. W. W. McDonald built the antebellum Old Stagecoach Stop, a preservation and heritage tourist site on the Waynesville square.

[7] Solomon King v. R. W. Wade, abatement, Phelps County circuit court, filed April 9, 1864, MSA.

[8] Walker and Henry Lick began a newspaper in 1859 in Vienna, but changed its name to the *Rolla Express* and moved it to Phelps County in 1860. *History of Cole, Moniteau, Morgan, Benton, Miller, Maries and Osage Counties, Missouri*, Chicago: Goodspeed Publishing Co., 1889, 614. In October 1863, the military arrested Henry Lick for publishing incendiary comments, closed the newspaper, and sent him to Gratiot Prison. The army later released Lick on his promise to not engage in newspaper publishing. Later, C. P. Walker reopened the *Rolla Express* office (copies are not available), and after the war Lick became a newspaper editor in Springfield, Greene County.

[9] Wade's torment is described in R. W. Wade v. Philip Jackson et al, false imprisonment, Phelps County circuit court, filed Sept. 6, 1864, MSA.

For the Man about to Lose His Job at Dillons

Marcus Cafagña

The barista turns up his brogue
as I wait at the counter for him
to pour my Americano with room.
Clouds of steam push up
around his rusty mutton chops,
coating his worry lines in sweat.
He's getting laid off
after Christmas, after he's done
tearing down the roaster,
the grinder, the espresso machine.
He's been working in the Ozarks
for a company in Kansas
owned by Kroger's in Ohio.
Because only this one market
turns a profit, every store
in the chain is closing.
The one that was across the street
is now a career center,
where folks like my friend
will file for unemployment.
Friend. That's what he calls
me today after he snaps
on the lid and I tip him and turn
to go, but I don't
even know his name.

The Present Past: Part II

We often fail to record the present past, extant things from earlier eras. Then they are gone. Old loft barns are a present past that will soon be the past. Several realities—the availability of custom-made metal buildings, changing farming practices, increased tax and insurance liability—have coalesced to increase their attrition rate. In the summer of 2005, I undertook to photograph all the loft barns in my home county, Dallas County, Missouri. I never finished the project, and many of the few dozen barns I photographed have collapsed or have been torn down. I also took a few photos of other structures, such as cabins and stores, which were sharing the same fate.

PDH

Doctrinally Unbound, Closer to Christ:
Harold Bell Wright's *The Calling of Dan Matthews*

John J. Han

INTRODUCTION

Harold Bell Wright's *The Calling of Dan Matthews* (1909) is a novel of religious satire along the lines of *The Decameron, The Canterbury Tales,* and other Western texts that attack the intolerance, hypocrisy, corruption, and doctrinal disputes within the institutional church. The main character of Wright's novel, Daniel Howitt Matthews, pastors a Protestant church in the Midwestern town of Corinth, most likely modeled after Lebanon, Missouri, where the author pastored the Christian Church (Disciples of Christ) from 1905-07. As soon as Dan arrives at his pastorate, he encounters difficulties posed by lay leaders and gossipers within the church. Disillusioned with the unwholesome environment of his church and the denomination, he renounces his ministry so that he can live by the moral teachings of Christ as a businessman. Thereafter, Dan dedicates his life serving needy people in the Ozarks, applying Christian principles to real-life situations.

Upon publication of *The Calling of Dan Matthews,* one of his five novels set in the Ozarks,[1] some readers, including pastors across the United States, denounced his harsh representation of the church. One year after the publication of *The Calling of Dan Matthews,* Alexander Corkey (1871-1914)—a clergyman born in Ireland—published a reactive novel, *The Victory of Allen Rutledge: A Tale of the Middle West* (Grosset & Dunlap). In this work, Corkey rebuts Wright's Christian vision by offering a different solution: instead of renouncing his pastoral vocation, Allen Rutledge stays to reform the church from within.

Despite the negative responses from many clerics and literary critics, *The Calling of Dan Matthews* was well received by the reading public, selling 925,000 copies.[2] In 1935, the novel was also made into a 67-minute movie by the same title. Produced by Columbia Pictures, this motion picture stars Richard Arlen (Dan Matthews), Charlotte Wynters (Hope Strong), and Douglass Dumbrill (Jeff Hardy). The popularity of *The Calling of Dan Matthews* suggests that the novel contains religious themes that resonate with its audience.

Written from a liberal Protestant's point of view, *The Calling of Dan Matthews* discards creedal Christianity in favor of a practical, humanistic, and humanitarian faith that addresses "the grim realities of life" (Wright, *Calling* 366). Christian faith envisaged by Wright reflects two religious influences on him: restoration theology (Christian primitivism) and the social gospel. Wright's negative view of doctrine-oriented theology was fostered by his affiliation with the Christian Church (Disciples of Christ), a branch of the American Restoration Movement that sought to unify all Christians in the spirit of the New Testament. Meanwhile, his emphasis on humanistic, humanitarian faith—faith in action—reflects the impact of the social gospel movement on him. This essay addresses the restoration theology and the social gospel as envisioned by the title character of the novel.

RESTORATIONISM AND THE SOCIAL GOSPEL MOVEMENT

The American Restoration Movement, which sought to restore simple Christianity sans theological trappings, arose during the Second Great Awakening of the early nineteenth century. This anti-denominational movement was spearheaded by a group of Protestant pastors, such as Barton W. Stone, Thomas Campbell, and his son Alexander Campbell. The Christian Church (Disciples of Christ), to which Harold Bell Wright belonged, came out of the Stone-Campbell Restoration Movement.

In his autobiography, *To My Sons* (1934), Wright discredits doctrinal Christianity as "denominational Christianity" and "churchianity" (207, 211). Not surprisingly, during his preaching ministry in Mount Vernon, Missouri, he was viewed with suspicion by both his fellow preachers, who had better credentials than he,[3] and lay leaders, who were puzzled by his avoidance of doctrinal matters. According to Wright, "[T]he reverend gentlemen [accepted] me with reservations," and the "wise old denominational elders [. . .] listened to my peculiar brand of preaching with somewhat pained expressions" (207). No wonder he did not wear a clerical robe, and he "abhorred being called 'reverend'" (207).

The social gospel movement began in the United States in the 1890s. Walter Rauschenbusch (1861-1918), a Baptist minister and professor at Rochester Theological Seminary, articulated the philosophical base for the movement in books such as *Christianity and the Social Crisis* (1907), *Christianizing the Social Order* (1912), and *A Theology of the Social Gospel* (1917). In *A Theology of the Social Gospel*, for instance, Rauschenbusch contends that overemphasis on the individualistic gospel overshadows institutional sinfulness: "It has not evoked faith in the will and power of God to redeem the permanent institutions of human society from their inherited guilt of oppression and extortion" (5). Deploring that the Kingdom of God was gradually replaced by the Kingdom of the Church after Jesus' death, Rauschenbusch advocates a return to Jesus' original vision of salvation. According to him, "The social gospel registers the fact that for the first time in history the spirit of Christianity has had a chance to form a working partnership with real social and psychological science. It is the religious reaction on the historic advent of democracy" (5).

It was Charles Sheldon, a Topeka, Kansas, pastor, who was instrumental in publicizing Rauschenbusch's social gospel. His novel *In His Steps: What Would Jesus Do?* (1896)—the best-known social-gospel novel—has sold several million copies and remains in print. Following in Sheldon's footsteps,[4] Harold Bell Wright championed the cause of the social gospel in some of his novels, including *That Printer of Udell's*, *The Calling of Dan Matthews*, *Helen of the Old House*, and *God and the Groceryman*.

ANTI-DENOMINATIONALISM AND THE SOCIAL GOSPEL IN WRIGHT'S NOVEL

In *The Calling of Dan Matthews*, organized, institutional religion is characterized by indoctrination, self-righteousness, hypocrisy, and denominational politics. The pervasive atmosphere is stifling and unforgiving. As a hired pastor of the Strong Memorial Church, Dan Matthews is not allowed to preach outside the denominational lines. Lay leaders, who are typically big donors, try to control Dan's life in minute detail, telling him what to do and what not to do although he does nothing against his conscience. He tries to please the lay leaders, which would guarantee continued employment, but eventually he leaves the church so that he can live in line with the basic teachings of Christ.

Gossip serves as a destructive weapon in Dan's congregation. The pastor's close relationship with Hope Farwell, who does not attend church, generates suspicions and rebukes from the laity. The church turns a blind eye to the unfortunate in the community; even when the church helps them, it has a self-serving motive. Interestingly, Dan does not find anyone within his church with whom he can have a genuine conversation about important life issues. His confidants are Dr. John Oldham, a retired physician in Corinth, and Hope Farwell, a nurse from Chicago. The two figures do not attend church, but they seem to be the only ones that understand him and care for him.

Dan's participation in a denominational convention exacerbates his disillusionment with institutionalized Christianity. At the convention, he has ample opportunities to observe the hunger for power that exists among pastors and lay leaders. In a particularly sardonic scene, Wright describes the different types of power-hungry people: the leaders, the would-be leaders, the self-constituted leaders, the heresy hunters, and the young preachers. The leaders cling to "the places of conspicuous honor and power" (Wright, *Calling* 363). The would-be leaders—"for the glory of Christ"—seek these "same seats of the mighty" (363). The self-constituted leaders try to make their presence known in hopes of achieving power within the denomination. The heresy hunters "[sniff] with hound-like eagerness for the scent of doctrinal weakness in the speeches of their brothers" (363). Finally, the young preachers "look with awe on the doings of the great ones, to learn how it was done and to watch for a possible opening whereby they might snatch their bit of glory here on earth" (363).

The seed of Dan's conversion to the social gospel is sown early in the novel through his association with Hope Farwell, who is a woman of compassion and self-confidence, and Dr. Oldham, who serves as his life mentor. One day, Dan and Hope have a contentious conversation about the role of ministers. She argues that the true church is *"inseparable from the religion of Christ"* (251; emphasis in original). According to her, Christ simply proclaimed the Kingdom of God; it was not his intention to found a religious institution to be controlled by men. She also states, "[The] selfish, wasteful, cruel, heartless thing that men have built up around their opinions, and whims, and ambitions, has so come between the people and the Christianity of the Christ" (252). When Dan provides a textbook answer by saying that "the minister is a servant of God" (252), Hope counters with a highly negative view of the Christian minister:

> To me he is the most useless creature in all the world. He is a man set apart from all those who live lives of service, who do the work of the world. And then that he should be distinguished from these world-workers, these servers, by this noblest of all titles—*a minister*—is the bitterest irony that the mind of the race ever conceived. (253)

When Dan says that the church employs a pastor as "minister to the world" (253), she replies that churches hire pastors for self-interested purposes, which apparently was not intended by Christ:

> [A] church employs a pastor to serve itself. To the churches Christianity has become a question of fidelity to a church and creed and not to the spirit of Christ. The minister's standing and success in his calling, the amount of his salary, even, depends upon his devotion to the particular views of the church that calls him and his ability to please those who pay him for pleasing them. (253)

In another part of the novel, Dr. Oldham reminds Dan of the disparity between Christ's teachings and the way churches are operated, saying that it requires courage to reform institutionalized Christianity which worships "a system" (387), not God. According to the doctor, "Every reformation begins with the persecution of the reformer and ends with the followers of that reformer persecuting those who would lead them another step toward freedom. Misguided religious people have always crucified their saviors and always will!" (385). Dr. Oldham encourages the young pastor to think big and become a pioneer in making this world truly better.

Clearly, Hope and Dr. Oldham embody Wright's social gospel, a lived gospel which Dan fully embraces later in the story. In his final sermon at the Memorial Church, Dan shares his renewed understanding of Christ's teachings, declaring that he has found a new mission outside the church:

> It is not the spirit of wealth, of learning, or of culture that can make the church of value, or a power for good in the world, but the spirit of Christ only. […] [The church] is holy to the degree that God is in it. God is as truly in the fields of grain, in the forests, in the mines, and in those laws of Nature by which men convert the product of field and forest and mine into the necessities of life. Therefore these are as truly holy as this institution. (390)[5]

CONCLUSIONS

In a sense, *The Calling of Dan Matthews* is a romantic story that portrays the beauty of the Ozark hills and dramatizes the blossoming love between the title character—a stout and handsome man—and Hope Farwell, "a beautiful woman [whose] womanhood [is] unspoiled by vain idleness, empty pleasures or purposeless activity" (346). On the other hand, Wright's novel is a naturalistic story that highlights the seamy side of church life. The novel is mainly on the shortcomings of the modern church and on how Christians can serve the world better. Not many positive things happen within the church and the denomination. As a preacher-novelist, Wright delivers the message that the traditional church needs to change because the followers of Christ are needed outside the walls of the church, not inside. By dealing with Christian themes that have universal implications, Wright makes his novel transcend its regional setting.

The Calling of Dan Matthews is a story of simple, stylized morality that relies on stock characters—the good guys and the bad guys. Yet, a hyperbolically negative representation of religion does not mean that there is not a grain of truth in it. To Wright's defense, one could argue that his novel allegorizes an American pastor who enters the ministry with good intentions but gradually realizes that the true church exists outside the brick-and-mortar church—among the common people who struggle with their own lives. The title of the novel implies that Dan Mathews is initially called to the pastoral ministry and then is eventually called out of the ministry as he seeks more effective ways to serve his neighbors. For him, the Kingdom of God, as preached by Jesus, is not something otherworldly but something that can be built on this earth.

In his conception of churches, Wright himself was not as radical as Dan Matthews, who resigns his pastoral position to live among the needy. After moving from Missouri to California, Wright took a pastoral position in 1907. In the same year, he resigned to write novels full time not because he was involved in some controversies within the church; he thought that writing was a form of Christian ministry in which he could reach a much wider audience. Also, he wrote his novel *That Printer of Udell's* while pastoring the Christian Church in Pittsburg, Kansas. The novel was enormously popular among his parishioners, which seems to imply that he was not someone who would stir doctrinal controversies in his church. Regardless, *The Calling of Dan Matthews* is an intriguing novel that is set in the socially conservative Midwest but promotes a vision of radically liberal Christianity.[6]

ENDNOTES

[1] The other four novels are *That Printer of Udell's: A Story of the Middle West* (1903), *The Shepherd of the Hills* (1907), *The Re-Creation of Brian Kent* (1919), and *Ma Cinderella* (1932). Although *God and the Groceryman* (1927) continues Dan Matthews's story, it is set in the Kansas City area, which is outside the Ozarks. Thus, the work can be considered a quasi-Ozarks novel.

[2] This number is based on Frank Luther Mott's rankings of bestsellers since 1665. According to Mott, five of Wright's novels sold at least 900,000 copies: 1.2 million for *The Shepherd of the Hills*, 925, 000 for *The*

Calling of Dan Matthews, 900,000 for *The Winning of Barbara Worth*, 925,000 for *The Eyes of the World*, and 965,000 for *When a Man's a Man* (Ferré 64).

[3] Wright had only a middle school education, but he self-educated through extensive reading.

[4] In *To My Sons*, Wright acknowledges that he borrowed the idea of reading *That Printer of Udell's* to his Pittsburg congregation from Charles Sheldon, who had read a chapter of *In His Steps* at a time to his Topeka congregation (211).

[5] Dan's sermon somewhat recalls the remarks of Jim Casy, the ex-preacher in Steinbeck's *The Grapes of Wrath* (1939), who has lost his sense of pastoral vocation and redirects his attention to those who are poor and dispossessed. In chapter 13 of the novel, Casy gives a public prayer, which is a pep talk by nature, at Grampa's funeral. Here, he affirms the moral imperative to help the needy:

> He's awright. He got a job to do, but it's all laid out for 'im an' there's on'y one way to do it. But, us, we got a job to do, an' they's thousan' ways, an' we don' know which one to take. An' if I was to pray, it'd be for the folks that don't know which way to turn. (148)

[6] An earlier version of this essay was presented at the 10th Annual Ozarks Studies Symposium, Missouri State University-West Plains, MO, 23-24 Sept. 2016.

WORKS CITED

Ferré, John P. *A Social Gospel for Millions: The Religious Bestsellers of Charles Sheldon, Charles Gordon, and Harold Bell Wright*. Bowling Green State University Popular Press, 1988.

Rauschenbusch, Walter. *A Theology for the Social Gospel*. Macmillan, 1917.

Steinbeck, John. *The Grapes of Wrath*. Viking, 1939.

Wright, Harold Bell. *The Calling of Dan Matthews*. 1935. *A Harold Bell Wright Trilogy: The Shepherd of the Hills, The Calling of Dan Matthew, God and the Groceryman*. Pelican Publishing, 2007, pp. 193-401.

———. *To My Sons*. Harper, 1934.

Childhood

Paulette Guerin

A crepe myrtle dangles
over the swimming hole:
brief, pink waves.

Buying the House

Paulette Guerin

Just children, we went to the bank too
because there was nowhere else for us to go.
Grandma handed Mother the down payment
wrapped in wrinkled foil.

She'd pulled it out of the deep freeze,
setting aside a hundred pounds of frozen venison,
bags of breaded okra and corn from the garden,
so we could have four walls all our own.

Green Grass of Home

C. D. Albin

With the tip of a forefinger, Ava slid the envelope an arm's length across her kitchen counter. There was no name of sender or return address, only a Little Rock postmark, but the message inside was indelible, heavy pen strokes scoring the paper in a left-handed scrawl still familiar despite the years: *In town for a while. Will drop by.* Cursing, she grabbed the envelope and shoved it elbow-deep in the overflowing trash can beneath the sink, then scoured her hands with hot water and dish soap before stalking out of the kitchen.

Ava reached her son's door ready to throttle him for letting her roses wilt, but the empty room robbed her of words. Orie had left a week ago Sunday in a fit of teenaged pique, a fact she found hard to accommodate now that he was living above Cliff Murchison's garage and doing odd jobs for him. The old man owned a rundown Victorian so sorry it made her eyes hurt, and she'd wasted an entire month trying to sell it for him. Eventually she low-balled the price in order to attract a buyer, but Murchison wouldn't go along. His stubbornness cost her a commission, not to mention a late fee on her mortgage. Remembering the bank's firmly worded notice, she clenched her teeth like a vise.

Suddenly the landline jangled throughout the house. Ava didn't recognize the number and grabbed her purse before locking the door behind her. Outside, the phone's faint, persistent ring followed her like a taunt until she slammed the door of her Civic and started the engine. She slumped back and massaged her eyelids, thinking through the to-do-list for the office, but phones rang there too. Muting her cell, she resolved that by noon she'd find at least one house she could talk someone into listing.

Ten minutes later she crested a hill in the old part of town and began casing residences as cannily as a burglar. She had known Belmont Street since childhood, white columns and heavy shade a legacy of Ozark gentry, but now the neighborhood was a mix of middle managers and hangers-on, those last the sort who believed their houses still carried a whiff of the family's prime. Ava doubted such people would open doors to her, but she scanned yards and driveways anyway, hoping for a clue that someone might be hard up. Near the end of the street she stopped in front of the neighborhood's only sore thumb, a late seventies split-level with twenty foot columns, the basement masquerading as a first floor. An unwashed Escape with a dented rear fender angled crookedly in the driveway.

Ava had a vague notion that the husband managed the local O'Reilly's, so she checked her face in the rearview, mussed her hair slightly, and started up the cracked walkway to the front door. There she banged a corroded brass knocker several times to no response. Turning to leave, she squinted across the street at a pearl white Queen Anne and knew instantly that to knock there would be pointless.

She was about to reach for her keys when a loud "Howdy!" froze her where she stood. A middle-aged woman carrying a pair of pruning shears turned the corner of the split-level and held the shears aloft as if Ava might want to examine them. "Just neatening up. Who are you?"

Ava flashed a smile she hoped was as bright as the house across the street. "Nice day for it. Cooler than it's been." She slipped a business card from the outer pocket of her purse and offered it to the woman. "Ava Fairchild Realty. Such a fine morning, I thought I should get out and visit."

The woman took the card as if it were an expired ticket stub. "Honey, we don't need an agent."

"It's a seller's market. You might be surprised."

The woman sighed, studied the card, and looked back at Ava. After a moment a dimple formed in her left cheek and her eyebrows arched. "Didn't you used to have an auctioneering business?"

Ava felt the slight incline of the walkway in the balls of her feet and fought an impulse to step back. When she was sure of her balance, she pointed her chin. "I've been helping people sell their homes for more than a year."

The woman nodded, fingers pulling at the damp bandanna around her neck. "I like pluck, Honey. But you lost your license, didn't you?"

Ava flashed back to a high school suspension she'd received for decking Billie Kaye Dozier, who had called her jailbait. "There's always two sides to a story," she said, her tone as flat as a postcard.

The woman pinched Ava's business card by one corner and handed it back. "That may be, but if people can't trust you with Grandma's old butter churn, why would they let you near their house?"

Heat flamed Ava's face and neck. She scrunched the card into a ball and choked an impulse to hurl it at the woman. "They let me near their house," she said, "because I'm going to be the richest real estate agent Bond County has ever seen."

The woman regarded her shears before pointing the tips toward the ground. "I don't mean offense. Troy says I'm subtle as a jack-hammer. But if I needed an agent, I'd want her to think about my bank account as much as hers."

Ava swept her eyes across the house's front façade, taking in worn-out window screens, spalling mortar, and a wasp's nest forming near the top of a column. "Lady, if I lived here, I'd bypass the agent and call somebody who's good with a bulldozer."

The woman's laugh began in her eyes and tremored down through her wattle. "Now there's professional advice," she said. "I guess I got mine for free." She gave the air two quick snips with her shears before resting them on a shoulder and starting toward the backyard. "You have a good day, Miss Ava Fairchild Realty."

Ava glared at the woman until she was out of sight, then turned on a heel and stomped toward the Civic, furious she'd amused someone she'd meant to rattle. As soon as she was out of the neighborhood she accelerated and began assembling a string of insults that would make the woman's smug face morph into tears. The vision held little solace though, and when Ava spotted a Burger King she swung into the drive-thru and shouted an order for a strawberry shake into the malfunctioning speaker. A teenage voice squawked back, insisting that shakes were not on the breakfast menu. Ava punched the steering wheel with the palm of her hand and sped away without reply.

When she arrived at the tiny fieldstone rental that served as her office, a midnight blue Silverado was parked like an omen in the middle of the single drive. She nudged the Civic close to the curb and got out, restraining her annoyance in case the driver might be a client. She had to pass close to the passenger door just to stay off the grass, but when she took a glimpse at the driver, she nearly dropped her keys. Steadying her fingers, she unlocked the door and decided against slamming it in his face, then fought a wilder impulse to blast his kneecap with the .32 nestled in her purse. Instead, she took measured steps across the snug anteroom to her office, settled herself behind the desk, and waited.

He stepped in whistling softly, a familiar melody she couldn't quite name. He tried to keep his boots quiet on the hardwood, but his gait was more thudding than she remembered, and his face was heavier too, a bit jowly now. Still, she could see Orie in him, a fact that pulled her heart in different directions. As he leaned against the door casing, she noticed his dark hair curled at the back of his collar. After a moment he moved his left hand like the sweep of a wiper blade. "Hey, Ava." When she stayed silent, he assumed a straighter posture. "Did you get my letter?"

"Eight words don't make a letter."

One side of his mouth stretched into a grin. "I save words for when they count."

"I bet."

He sighed and pointed to one of the chairs facing her desk. When she didn't say no, he sat down, a hint of cologne invading the air. "How you been?"

"What do you want, Arlen?"

He shrugged and turned up his palms, making a show of looking around the room. "Real estate, right? Thought you could find me a house."

She scooted back and began paging through an appointment book. "Be serious."

"I am, Ava."

"You'll never leave Kentucky."

"I could keep a second place down here on the lake."

"Lake houses cost more than you think."

He arched his shoulders against the back of the chair and crossed his legs. "I'm doing okay. And I don't need anything big. Maybe two bedrooms." He tilted his head. "Someplace Orie could stay if he wanted."

The dates in the appointment book blurred briefly. She blinked and looked to the corner of her desk, where she kept a picture of Orie and his brother Paul. "No."

"He's my son. He's eighteen."

"He'll come to no good around you."

"I could say the same to you."

"I fed and raised him. Kept a roof over him."

Arlen leaned forward. "Sounds like you're afraid he'd consider it." He traced a forefinger along the edge of her desk. "Every boy needs a father."

"You're no father. Just a dick in cowboy boots."

A full grin split his face and he reclined again, lifting a boot toward the corner of her desk. "Then you'll love this pair of Justins I bought—"

Ava shot forward and caught his heel a half inch before it touched wood, jerking the leg as high as her shoulder. Arlen's chair upended, dumping him on the floor. By the time he cursed and scrambled up she was wrist-deep in her purse, and she knew from the tempering in his eyes that he heard the hammer of the .32 beneath her thumb. "Go home, Arlen."

He grimaced and rubbed an elbow. "I'm here to see my boy."

"He's seen enough of you."

Arlen dropped his gaze to her purse. "You still have that old pop gun?"

"It'll do the job," she said, letting her weight settle into a hip. "That's why you gave it to me."

He shook his head. "This is wrong, Ava."

The way he said "wrong" struck her as funny, as if he found the word hard to pronounce. "Wrong will happen if I catch you near Orie," she said, then lowered her voice and added, "or if Paul does."

Arlen blew air through his nose and retreated a step, resting both hands on his belt. "So you still have Hercules under your thumb."

"Paul makes his own choices."

"Sure he does."

Ava's palm felt moist against the butt of the revolver. "You've been told, Arlen."

"Then don't bring Paul into it."

"He's my son, same as Orie."

"He's not mine."

Ava couldn't keep a smile from playing at the corners of her mouth. "Then tell Paul to stay out of your business," she said, and slowly lowered the hammer of the .32. "You want his address?"

By early afternoon Ava was pent up and fidgety sitting alone in her little office. Arlen had slunk away hours ago, and Michelle, the part-time receptionist newly arrived from Iowa, was out with allergies and didn't think she would be at work for the rest of the week. Glancing up, Ava noticed the starburst clock she'd salvaged from her auctioneering business had stopped again, its stalled hands mocking her sense of wasted time. She tried to forget Arlen and what he might be plotting, but it was no use, so she dialed Orie's number hoping he would pick up. After several rings the call went to voicemail, as it had all week. Irked, she threw her half-eaten sandwich in the trash and made sure the answering machine was on before locking the office.

She hated going to Murchison's just to talk to her son, but she didn't see how to avoid it. If she could make her way up the rickety stairs to the apartment without attracting attention from the house, she could warn Orie that Arlen was back and be gone before the old man knew she was around. The last time she'd been at the property she had tangled with Murchison's hysterical daughter, who threatened to get a restraining order. Ava didn't care for more drama like that.

When she pulled alongside the curb in front of Murchison's house, Ava spotted Orie's pickup parked beside the garage, then contemplated a wide patch of siding along the front of the house where paint had been scraped down to bare clapboards. *So he even has you painting his house*, she thought, fingers tightening on the steering wheel while she worried that if Orie could be manipulated by some-one like Murchison, he would stand no chance against a first rate gaslighter like Arlen.

Biting her lip, she regarded the stairs on the side of the garage like a prize at the end of a gauntlet. To reach them she needed to pass beneath a grove of oaks and cross thirty feet of open ground before arriving at the garage. Taking a deep breath, she left the Civic and hugged her purse close. Three-inch heels kept her from breaking into a jog, but she walked quickly, grateful to Orie for hacking down the overgrown yard. Emerging from the deep shade of the oaks, she turned toward the garage just as Murchison stepped onto his porch and did a double-take at her appearance. After a moment he called toward the back yard, then eyed her until Orie came to the front of the house.

Orie gave her one glance as he mounted the porch, then positioned himself beside Murchison and mumbled something in the old man's ear. Ava's resentment flared. "Hey," she shouted, striding nearer the porch. "You don't say hello to your mother?"

A moment passed before Orie looked in her direction. Squaring his shoulders, he descended the steps and came close enough that she could have touched him, his dark eyes drilling down into hers. "I'm not leaving."

"Did I say you were?"

"And let Cliff alone."

Ava spiked a heel into the dry lawn. "What?"

"Let him alone. He hasn't done anything to you."

She jerked her purse strap higher on her shoulder. "That's not what I'm here to talk about."

"Then go on home."

Ava spotted Murchison lingering near his front door and lowered her voice. "Are you going to listen to me or not?"

"Not," he said, and started for his pickup.

Ava hurried after him, unwilling to aim words at his back. When he reached for the door handle she threw herself in front of him. "You get ahold of your temper," she shouted, but knew immediately that she'd thrown kerosene on fire.

"Move," he said.

She tried to stay between him and the door, but he was too strong and opened it hard against her. Stumbling, she grabbed the crook of his elbow. "Arlen's back," she cried. Orie's body went as straight as a cornerpost, and when he didn't pull away, she tightened her grip.

Ava knew where they were going when Orie turned down the narrow lane that led to People's Pavilion, the picnic area where she had brought him to play as a child. He drove to the back of the nearly deserted lot and parked in the shade of a tall pin oak. Ava waited, listening to random ticks of the engine until he asked, "How long has he been back?"

She caught him glance her way, then pull out his phone. "I don't know," she said. "He just showed up at my office this morning."

He began scrolling messages. "So what's he want?"

She nodded. "That's the right question. Anytime you deal with him, ask yourself that."

"I'm not dealing with him. I won't even cross his path."

"You say that, but Lotten is small."

"I'll see him coming."

"I used to think that too."

Orie gave her an appraising stare. "You two have a go round this morning?"

"Not really." She studied the timbered ridge beyond the parking lot. "I named Paul to him before anything started."

Orie laughed quietly. "I guess that paused him."

"Pretty much." She stifled an urge to grab Orie's hand, hold it as tightly as she did when he was little. "Don't think that ends it though."

Orie shrugged. "Paul's a truck you point downhill. He'd turn Arlen into a grease puddle."

"Don't talk like that. I don't control your brother."

"Sure."

Ava glanced at her palms, wondering what a fortune teller might read there. "You're too smart for your own good." When he smirked, she took a hard swipe at her bangs. "Have you turned in that application to Ozark Mountain yet?"

"They take anybody," he said, and reached for the ignition. "They'd let me in during finals week."

"Who told you that?"

"I've got time."

"If you're counting on time, you're not as smart as you think."

Orie punched the gas, tires squalling as he peeled out in reverse. "You're the one who thinks I'm smart," he shouted, then bullied the pickup into gear before gunning it toward the highway.

Orie dropped Ava off where she had parked at Murchison's curb, and before she could touch her door handle the pickup snarled down the quiet street and vanished around the curve. She shook her head and slid behind the wheel, scowling toward the Victorian half hidden in the trees. Nobody could tell her Murchison didn't owe her money, at least for her time. And Orie staying here was an insult, one that set her teeth on edge.

Suddenly bitterness jabbed her like a spur and she left the car in a bee-line for Murchison's front door. The third time she knocked, the old man stepped out as if emerging from a cave, gray eyes squinting in the afternoon glare. "Ms. Fairchild."

"I'm here to talk about Orie," she blurted.

Murchison sighed and motioned toward a pair of peeling rockers. "What's on your mind?"

Ava swept her eyes along the clapboards, wondering how much time Orie had spent scraping them. "This is a warning," she said. "Don't take advantage."

Choosing the far rocker, Murchison lowered himself stiffly. "Orie's a good worker."

"Then you better pay him like one."

The old man looked out at his yard as if he were trying to see across a lake. "We have an agreement. He does maintenance around here, he stays for free. Long as he's enrolled at the junior college."

"He's not enrolled."

Murchison angled the rocker in her direction. "Day before yester-day," he said, brushing something from the knee of his trousers. "Took him myself."

"Why didn't he tell me that?"

"I don't know. You could ask him."

Heat broke onto the surface of her skin. "I'll do that. And don't think I've forgotten what you did to me with this house. I'm going to sue the pants off you."

Murchison arched furry eyebrows before bending and carefully hiking each pant leg to display skinny, blue-veined calves. "Always thought I had nice legs," he said. "What's your opinion?"

Ava skipped a return trip to the office and went straight home. In the medicine cabinet she found two Tylenols and washed them down with a flat-tasting Coke, then fixed a peanut butter and jelly sandwich. Afterward, the silence of the house took on an accusing tone, and she realized that of all the things Orie had seemed to be this afternoon—rude, angry, arrogant, stubborn—homesick hadn't been one of them.

For twenty minutes she tried distracting herself with the newscast out of Jonesboro, but when she caught herself channel surfing, she tossed the remote to the far end of the couch and assaulted her bedroom closet, filling two grocery boxes with scuffed, down-at-the-heel pumps, out-of-date blouses, and several pairs of jeans she couldn't have pried herself into with a crowbar. When she finished, she collapsed onto the bed and tried to nap, but her mind ping-ponged between the mocking lady on Belmont and Arlen being his asinine self at her office. The tune he had whistled kept running through her head, but she couldn't place it until the line "They'll all come to meet me" spoke itself in her memory. Exasperated, she pictured Porter Wagoner bedazzled in rhinestones while he crooned about some doomed prisoner and the family he'd never see. It was vintage Arlen, playing the victim for all he was worth.

The next morning at her office, Ava cold called with a vengeance, ringing acquaintances and inflating by thousands the likely value of their homes. She endured two hours of gruff refusals and sour "no thank you's," but finally there was a cautious "we'll see" from a retired principal fed up with operating a Christmas tree farm. Encouraged, she took a break and swirled coffee crystals into a cup of hot water, musing that if she had to close her doors, she could at least find work at a call center. As if on cue, the landline rang and she jumped for it, hoping for a callback. The voice on the line was Arlen's.

"Hey, Wildcat," he drawled.

"Don't call me that."

"Okay, but Ava's an old lady's name."

She splashed the coffee into the sink and stalked back to her desk. "You just drip with charm, don't you?"

"Some think I do."

"Say what you want, Arlen, or you'll be on Medicare before you talk to me again."

He cleared his throat into her ear. "Like I said yesterday. I'm looking for a house on the lake. Be a nice commission, wouldn't it?"

Ava clenched her eyes and imagined tiny veins straining on the insides of her lids.

"Hey? You there?"

"I told you no."

"You can change your mind."

"Why would I?"

"Because it's easy money."

Ava glanced at the picture of her sons. "You mean dirty money."

"When's money ever been dirty to you? Besides, I earned this clean."

"How?"

"You remember old Henry Ketchum?"

"He's as greasy as you are!"

A snicker vibrated on the other end of the line. "We're partners now. Payday loans. You ought to get in yourself."

Ava's mood dropped to her shoe tops. She hadn't sold a house in four months and couldn't have invested in a side business if she wanted to, but she'd rather be bitten by bats than admit such a thing to Arlen. "I'm doing fine," she said, sticking out her chin. "People will know this business."

"You mean like they knew the last one? You made the *Ledger*, Ava. Page one."

Her stomach churned as she pictured Arlen cackling at a computer screen back in Kentucky, probably charging an online subscription just to read more about how she'd lost her auctioneer's license. She wanted to strangle the man, but such intimate harm meant she'd have to touch him. "I'm busy, Arlen. I work for a living."

"If you'd listen you wouldn't have to work so hard. I'm practically throwing money at you."

Ava rolled her eyes. "Arlen, you're as see-through as a window. You're after Orie and you think you can buy him, but you don't know a thing about him."

"So whose fault is that?"

Ava moved the phone in front of her face and stared. "Seriously? You like listening so much, you listen to this!" She brought the receiver down hard on the corner of the desk and began pounding, parts from the keypad popping past her head like bits of shrapnel. When she tired, she tossed what was left of the phone in the trash and collapsed into the nearest chair, calculating that her temper had just cost her twenty bucks for a replacement phone at Walmart. The amount was small, but it hurt like a punch to the kidney.

For the rest of the day Ava rattled around her office getting nothing done. In the middle of the afternoon she went out for errands and returned to find a sizeable shoebox on the front stoop. A note duct-taped to one corner bore the scrawled message, "Something for Orie. You weirded out before I could explain."

Ava's instincts told her to toss the box in the dumpster, but the contents felt substantial. Inside her office she set the box in the middle of her desk and pondered the novelty of Arlen as a benefactor. He'd never given Orie anything of value except looks, but experience taught her how chancy it was to act as his go-between. When her protective impulses finally got the best of her, she snatched the lid off the box and eyed a new pair of Justin boots, their leathery aroma entering the room like a presence. "That figures," she growled, recalling the gleaming pair Arlen had worn yesterday, then savoring the memory of him floundering on the floor of her office. She had never seen Arlen so flustered, and pride warmed her like good brandy.

A few minutes before closing time, Ava locked her office and drove two blocks to the sparsely graveled lot of Osage Roofing, where she parked near Paul's Bronco. Hoping for a breeze, she lowered her window before glancing at the boot box on the seat beside her, uncertain whether Paul would do what she asked. Orie might think she controlled his older brother like a puppet, but there was no guarantee with Paul.

Eyes on the back door, Ava watched the office manager and two roofers leave one by one before Paul came out wearing a filthy white T-shirt and grimed jeans. He hitched a step when he spotted her, then resumed an end-of-day plod in her direction. At her window he stiff-armed the Civic's roof and leaned down. "Been expecting you."

"Why?"

"Figured you'd be after me to drag Orie back."

"He'll be back."

Paul shifted his weight. "Okay."

Ava cut her eyes toward ditch weeds at the edge of the parking lot. "This isn't about Orie," she said. Beyond the weeds a tiny dust devil formed, then fell apart so quickly she doubted she'd seen it. "I mean, we need to keep it from being about Orie."

Paul shook his head. "Say that in English."

She watched his face for the storm that would come. "Arlen's back."

For a moment Paul didn't move, then the car rocked as he pushed himself upright. "He's better off in Kentucky."

"I told him that."

"He listen?"

"I don't think so." She removed the lid of the boot box. "He left these at my office. For Orie."

Paul peered through her window. "Shiny."

Ava felt a dart of fear prick her heart. "Sometimes Orie takes to shiny."

"He seen them yet?"

"No."

Paul straightened again, wafting a whiff of dried sweat. "Tell him they're from you. A graduation present."

"He wouldn't believe that."

"Then what?"

Ava swallowed. "I thought you could take them back to Arlen. Tell him to leave Orie alone."

After a moment Paul reached a thick arm through the window. "Hand 'em here."

She replaced the box lid but Paul swept it off, studying the boots as if committing them to memory. Slowly his seamed lips parted and he smiled. "Wish they were bigger," he said. "I could wear 'em while I kick his ass."

After three days Paul called to report he'd found no sign of Arlen. "Can't even sniff old stink," he complained. Ava convinced him to keep looking, then leaned back in her office chair and considered the odds her ex-husband had left town on his own. His departure would be a jackpot, but she'd never won more than ten dollars on a scratchers ticket and doubted her luck would be better now. Arlen had a knack for catching her off guard, especially when her defenses were low, and she bit her lip recalling ways he had torpedoed her in the past. There was the time she had thrown him out for cheating and he wouldn't stop calling, plying her with hurt puppy pleas as weepy as a Hank Williams song. She had fallen for it, but a week after letting him back in her bed she caught him tickling a topless blonde on the front seat of his truck, just around the corner from their rent house. Yet even that episode hadn't hurt as much as outright theft, like the time he pried the lock on an old jewelry box her grandmother had left her, pocketing the money she'd saved for classes at Ozark Mountain. After that it took nearly a decade for her to earn credits for a real estate license, and to this day she averted her eyes anytime she drove past the campus, as if the sight might scald her retinas.

Ava shook her head and told herself she had to get on with here and now. For the rest of the morning she played phone tag with the guy who wanted out of the Christmas tree business, finally setting 11:30 to meet him for photos. By 1:00 she was back at her office, sweaty from tromping past rows of evergreens and paranoid that ticks were roaming beneath her clothes. She had just begun to upload the photos when the front door swung open, and she saw with a pang that it was Arlen.

He feigned sheepishness as he entered, removing his cap to cross the anteroom, but when he reached her office he straightened and began whistling the same old Porter Wagoner tune that had run through her head all week.

"Don't you know any other songs?" she snapped.

He warbled through the rest of the chorus before leaning farther into the room. "It's a classic. 'Green, Green Grass of Home.'"

"He dies at the end, Stupid."

Arlen gave her a lopsided grin and hunched his shoulders. "But he's home."

She spread her hands flat on the desk, trying for calm. "Why are you here?"

Arlen tugged the lobe of his ear and glanced around the room. "Got wind Paul was looking for me." His eyes stopped at the copy machine, where she had set her purse when she came in. "Figured you sent him."

"You shouldn't figure. You'll wear yourself out."

"Ha," he said, taking a moment to settle the cap on his head. "Looks like I figured close enough to dodge him." He came forward and planted knobby knuckles on her desk. "Got you alone, too."

Ava felt a lightness in her temples. She willed herself not to glance at her purse, but the cell phone lay next to her hand and she palmed it, rolling her chair back and punching a quick text to Paul. When Arlen leaned in, she lowered the phone to her lap.

"What's that about?" he asked, his voice rasping like spilled gravel.

The tone annoyed her and she shoved the phone close to his face, forcing him to squint as he read the words, "He's here."

"Who's it to?"

"Who do you think?"

Before she could move, Arlen's left hand struck like a scythe and the phone crashed against the wall.

Instantly Ava's thumb throbbed, but she quelled an impulse to slap back. "That'll cost you," she said, proud she could keep her tone level, like someone powerful enough to control an outcome.

Arlen darkened. "Send me the bill."

Her voice lurched higher. "I'm through with bills. Paul will take it out of your hide."

Arlen thrust a middle finger in her direction as he turned for the door. She grabbed her purse and followed, then ran back and scooped up her phone, texting Orie to see if the device still worked. Suddenly a screech of tires on the street outside made her catch her breath. When she reached the stoop, Paul's Bronco was nosed inches from the grill of the Silverado. A moment later Arlen came hustling around the tailgate with Paul close behind. The two men scrambled onto the smudge of lawn before Paul hooked Arlen by the belt and took him down as if he were a child. Arlen kicked out with his boots until Paul leaned into the lashing legs and shouldered them away, dropping a knee into Arlen's ribs. A yowl broached the air and made Ava reach for her throat, but her son drove a single blow into the other man's face and the struggle ceased.

Paul came toward her, breathing hard. "Worthless piece of crap," he huffed.

Ava hiked her purse onto her shoulder. "He was about to pull something on me."

"Pull what?"

She shook her head and watched Arlen struggle to his feet. With a handkerchief he made cautious passes at his nose, then scowled toward the stoop as if the two of them were playground bullies. "I'll sue," he wheezed.

Paul bolted from the stoop with such force, the decking bounced beneath Ava's feet. She followed him into the yard and reached for an arm. "No more. Let him alone."

"You better ride that truck back to Kentucky," Paul shouted.

Arlen wagged a finger in retreat. "Listen to your mama."

"You backtalk me, I'll let the air out of you."

Arlen gasped as he hauled himself into the cab a limb at a time. "You already done that."

"I mean it," Paul barked. "You spark that thing now."

"Damn it, come away," Ava pleaded. "We want him gone."

Instead, Paul primed himself, fists tensing like heartbeats. Then a rich rumble poured from the Silverado's engine. Ava looked to the cab, where she saw Arlen's eyes had narrowed to slits. Suddenly an ache arced across her jawbone, lighting her memory like a fuse. "No!" she yelled, but the Silverado bulled over the curb and tore a tight arc in the sod as it spun toward them. Paul sent her sailing with a shove, then crouched and spun, taking the brunt of the blow in his left hip. Bowled like a barrel across the lawn, he stopped himself after the third roll and rose painfully to one knee, cursing the bloody scrape running the underside of his forearm.

By the time Ava regained her feet, Arlen had maneuvered the truck to face them, his head moving in a slow, satisfied bob as if to music. Livid, Ava snatched the .32 from her purse and stalked the pickup, savoring Arlen's yelp as he ducked beneath the dashboard. She put two rounds into the grill before raising her aim and blasting the windshield multiple times, cracked glass spiraling around each bullseye of a hole. After several moments, Arlen tumbled out of the passenger's side door and scrambled on all fours to shield himself behind Paul's Bronco.

Lowering the pistol, Ava felt her body lighten, as though every bone had hollowed like a bird's. She took a deep breath, and when Arlen's curses reached her, she laughed, rising on her toes as though the next breeze might lift her elsewhere. Then she heard her own voice mocking Arlen in song. "Yes, they'll all come to greet me," she crooned, "when they lay me 'neath the green, green grass of home." Blocks away in the middle of town a siren wailed, and she looked to Paul, who ceased cleaning his arm with a reddened shirttail. But Ava continued to sing, waving the pistol in rhythm until finally someone wrapped strong hands around hers, guiding her exhausted arms to her sides. Slowly she realized the person holding her was Orie, sweet son come from nowhere to lift this burden from her grasp.

Come Again, Carolina Wren
(for Allison Sloan)

Gerry Sloan

Can a lone wren depend on
the kindness of strangers
to get us through the winter,
hopping about, reconnoitering

the changeable terrain?
Or is it we who depend on
this nervous bird for stability,
this skittery citizen intent

on scouting its environment?
If I were on the other side
of this window looking in,
too old or lazy to migrate,

what would I see? An aging man
in a woolen sweater, equally
uncertain of the future, restlessly
foraging for words instead of silage,

a pioneer like yourself whose ancestors
kept questing westward, until they
arrived in this place that seemed
as if it couldn't be bested.

Tuning the Melon
(for Lester Monts)

Gerry Sloan

Not his scholarly
prowess or trumpet chops
I recall tonight, cutting

the season's first
watermelon, but his foolproof
test: thumping it

three times: the resounding
Low B-flat, second line
bass clef, a note I had played

a thousand times on trombone,
Lester's infallible proof
of ripeness. So here I share

the secret with my wife,
who nods in agreement
(for once in my life),

his Africa, her China, my Ozarks—
a colliding thump,
a sweetness.

Those Little Brown Cows

Jim Hamilton

Once upon a time we milked little brown cows, rather than big black and white ones.

When I was a small boy in the early 1950s, docile, doe-eyed Jerseys dominated Ozarks pastures, joined by that other Channel Island breed, Guernseys with their big, white spots on coats of amber brown. Both produced gallons of rich yellow milk that was markedly higher in butterfat and had more nonfat nutrients than that of today's dominant breed, the familiar Holstein-Freisan.

Jerseys had the edge over their taller cousins with milk routinely testing over 5 percent butterfat, but Guernseys were almost as high, producing what was once marketed as "Golden Guernsey" milk.

Jerseys were the rule on our small dairy, though Guernseys, Ayrshires, Brown Swiss, and Milking Shorthorns were not uncommon. Tagging along with my dad, an artificial inseminator (AI) — or "cow breeder," as they were commonly called — I became familiar with dairy herds of all breeds in the 1950s. Most were small herds on small farms, milked twice daily in quaint stanchion barns dating to the pre-war era of cream separators. In my day, though, most were selling whole milk for manufacturing cheese and butter.

By the time I was big enough to slide under the business end of a cow, though, we sold whole milk strained into 10-gallon cans and carried to the road for the milk hauler to pick up every morning. I never had anything to do with a cream separator, but I was quite familiar with cream.

Only at school did I drink "blue john" homogenized and pasteurized milk from little waxed cartons. To a boy accustomed to raw milk poured from a jar with several inches of thick cream on the top, processed milk was a bland liquid made palatable only with the addition of chocolate flavoring.

"Real milk" was what we produced at home, and the thick, yellow cream was a delicacy over wild blackberries, peaches, strawberries, chocolate cake or anything else that today might be decorated with soy-based whipped topping.

Folks today would say raw, whole milk is an acquired taste—if they could be persuaded to try it. Conversely, after leaving home as a teen, I had to get used to store-bought milk. Only in recent years have I come to accept the 2 percent variety, and that reluctantly. Oh, how far I've fallen from my Jersey days!

Like most of my farm experience, the dairy of my youth was a throwback to that of an earlier generation. Though grade A barns were cropping up in the Ozarks like daisies on overgrazed pastures, and colored breed cows were rapidly being replaced with black and white ones, Dad stuck with Jerseys for as long as he sold milk. His foundation animals were all registered Jerseys from bloodlines familiar in the postwar years. A pioneer in AI, Dad brought his work home with him. He both preached and practiced improving genetics.

In later years we had one Guernsey cow, aptly named "Guernsey," in a herd of Jerseys of much better temperament than their leggy cousin. A few years after I left home, Dad also had one black and white cow. That was shortly before new dairy barn requirements in the early 1970s put him out of the business. For years thereafter, though, Dad kept a cow for house milk.

Though Dad always advocated for Jersey cows, he was no stranger to Holsteins. I was around six years old when he worked for Maplewood Farms at Nixa — that was between his MFA bull farm and Curtiss breeding days — and I saw the biggest Holstein cow I'd ever seen. If memory serves me, she was from the Carnation dairy stock, an impressive animal.

Today I realize the cow I saw led around on the green turf at Maplewood was a vision of the future. A big change was afoot.

A few years ago, I had the opportunity to visit with Dr. John Underwood, author of *Sires of Distinction*, MFA Incorporated's 2012 book on the history of the MFA bull farm near Springfield and the early AI industry. Underwood notes that eighteen of the first bulls brought to the farm in the late 1940s were Jerseys. Another ten were Guernseys, and just four were Holsteins.

Over ensuing decades the ratio of black and white to brown changed dramatically. By the 1980s brown cows were becoming a rarity on Ozarks farms, while black and white dominated the struggling industry. But color has not been the greatest change in the dairy landscape. Dairy cow numbers of all breeds today are just a shadow of what many of us remember from our youth. In 2000, the number of dairy cows in Missouri was 154,000. By 2021 the count was 71,000, though the state still ranked 25th in the nation.

Numbers, however, don't tell the whole story.

For many of us who grew up on small farms in the 1950s and 1960s, dairy farming was all about the cows. Those little brown Jerseys we milked all had names. They were family. Each had a personality. We could put our hands on them. They were as much pets as our bluetick and beagle hounds.

I suppose it was different on big, grade A dairies. But to be fair, I knew some folks who had black and white cows just as spoiled rotten as our Jerseys. Bucket calves seem to turn out that way.

A few days ago, I talked with a Century Farm owner who also grew up milking Jersey cows by hand, though many more than we had. His family milked 90 head twice a day.

All they ever milked were Jerseys, and when high butterfat didn't count for much, they quit.

I don't know if I could be quite as sentimental about that many brown cows. We never had more than eight or ten.

But I still sometimes wish I had a quarter-cup of Jersey cream to pour over Martha's chocolate cake.

I don't much wish, though, that I had a cow to milk every night and morning.

Guess the good old days are better remembered than re-lived.

Remembering the River of Used to Be

Jim Hamilton

Several years ago I penned a tribute to my River of Used to Be — a mile or two of the Pomme de Terre near Fair Grove.

As I cross that same river today, I see little to remind me of the sparkling Ozarks stream of my youth. Rather, I see it fading even deeper into the hazy mist of the past.

It may yet be a beautiful stream, viewed from the deck of a high bridge; but, when I was a boy I could dip my hands in its cool water, wade its riffles and follow its deep eddies from above the Lost Bridge to near the U. S. 65 bridge.

How blest I was to know the Pomme de Terre when we could simply pull our pickup truck off the road and walk a few steps down to the water for a few minutes or hours of angling for black perch, goggle-eye, or smallmouth bass. How precious are memories of sitting at night on a gravel bar above Potter's Ford with my dad and brothers, our lines cast into a deep, dark abyss in hopes of catching fat bullhead catfish.

The bridge that now spans the river a few yards below the site of the former low-water crossing offers no access to the water, but simply a scenic view of the convergence of two streams with the river and a view of the former swimming hole that welcomed generations of farm youth on hot summer days. The relocated, paved county road affords no access to our former fishing holes down well-beaten paths, nor entry to an old farm road alongside pastures below the ford.

No matter. Fences now bar entry to places we once frequented. New houses have been built where none stood in my youth. Old footpaths to and along the river are long gone. Once far removed from town, the whole area seems a suburb of Fair Grove. The farmers who once had no qualms with a few local folks crossing the edges of field to get to the fishing holes must have passed on or sold their farms to a generation of different fabric. Even if not, I understand the fences. Visitors to the river may be of a different cloth than I remember, too. If the litter I pick up along the road by my house is any indication of the degree of the disrespect the river and her bordering landowners are shown, I marvel little at fences and posted properties.

Much about the river is different from when I was a boy — even the fishing. It started with the completion of Pomme de Terre Lake in the 1960s. The big fish seemed to leave, and the upper reaches of the river teemed with small bass and carp. As a fishery, it was never the same. In retrospect, I suppose my River of Used to Be was but a moment in time, as was my youth.

I've not fished the river near Fair Grove for years. Maybe it's better, now. I could probably get permission to cross a fence or two and find out, but I doubt it would be worth it.

I'd rather just remember the river as it was.

How sweet the memory of wading that cold, clear stream 60 years ago and coaxing big perch, goggle-eye, and feisty smallmouth from swirling eddies below midstream boulders.

How blest I was to love my River of Used to Be when I was but a boy, and even more to have it love me back.

Before We Had Duct Tape

Jim Hamilton

I came into some unexpected treasure a few weeks before Christmas—wire-tied hay bales.

After several years of relying on rusty wads hanging in forgotten corners of the barn, we have a fresh supply of baling wire.

Wire-tied bales used to be common on Ozarks farms, therefore an ample supply of wire. But in recent years fewer square bales have been tied with wire than with hemp or plastic twine, and small square bales have largely been replaced by big, round bales.

At the same time, farms have generally been replaced by housing subdivisions, too—but that's fodder for a different day. This is about baling wire.

Before duct tape held the world together, baling wire did the job.

When I was a boy growing up on the farm, baling wire was almost as indispensable as the hay it bound into bales.

It kept most of the place from falling apart. If we hadn't had baling wire as a natural byproduct of farming, no telling what kind of a mess we'd have been in.

Our old, rusty barbed wire fences wouldn't have held a broken-down milk cow, if not for baling wire to mend the breaks and hold the gates.

Any size or series of breaks could be fixed with enough baling wire. Wrapped around the post, it also sufficed to hold things in place where a rusty staple (or "steeple," as we called 'em) had fallen out of a rock-hard, spindly oak or hedge post.

Maybe it didn't make for the fanciest fence in the county, but it cost next to nothing at all, it was what we had, and it did the job—at least 'til next time.

No handier a repair kit was ever invented than a pair of pliers and a wad of baling wire in the back pocket of a pair of overalls, the newer and more pliable the wire, the better.

Just about anything could be fixed with wire and pliers.

Working on old cars and trucks, we discovered that a tin can with both ends cut out and split along the seam made a passable patch for a muffler or tailpipe. Baling wire, of course, became the clamp to hold it on.

A few tight wraps of wire around a broken hoe handle could make it almost as good as new. A generous wrap of tape over the wire made it even better—a little easier on the hands. What we generally used was that sticky, black friction tape. I don't recall ever seeing a roll of gray duct tape when I was a boy.

In desperation I once tied up a floppy shoe sole with loops of baling wire twisted tight and cut. It didn't look too fashionable, but it got me through a day of school. With their penchant for poking pins and wires through their noses, ears, eyebrows and other body parts, some teens today might wish they had a pair of my baling wire brogans. Wonder if that fellow Doc Martens is in the phone book?

Our most fortuitous employ of baling wire came one night when we'd gone fishing down on the Pomme de Terre and the tie rod end dropped off our '48 Ford pickup as we were turning around to leave.

Dad retrieved a length of baling wire from under the truck seat, pulled the long-nosed pliers from his overalls (the same pliers he used for peeling the skins off of catfish), crawled under the truck and wired it all back together.

In less than 10 minutes, we were on the road and headed home—not at breakneck speed, but not walking, either. Baling wire saved the night.

The possibilities of baling wire are endless. It's really a lot better than duct tape. It's like string, but a lot stronger, stiffer and tougher. Just think of all the uses we have for string (I guess we'd have to draw the line at flying kites. I can't imagine using baling wire in place of kite string, but it might be used to tie two crossed sticks into a frame).

As a rule, we used it to tie or hang most anything. From baling wire I could fashion a new link in a broken dog chain, make a tie to close a gunny sack, a latch for any gate on the place, or a tie down for a tarp over the hay.

Its applications are as infinite as an Ozarker's ingenuity.

I'm proud to again have some around.

It could prove even luckier than a buckeye in my pocket.

Before the Lakes Came In

Jim Hamilton

If you are in your 70s, you were born into an Ozarks landscape much different from today's.

You came in before the big Corps of Engineers lakes.

At 74 I remember many of the Missouri Ozarks' free-flowing streams and rivers. I was small, but I remember.

My dad was a consummate fisherman, taking every opportunity he had to drop a line in the water between AI calls to Southwest Missouri farms. The eldest of his four sons, I often rode with him on his backroads calls in the early 1950s. Along with his cow-breeder kit, kit, he always carried fishing tackle and poles in the trunk.

Of course, I may not remember the Ozarks of the early 1950s as clearly as someone 10 years my senior, but I still recall the infancy of today's bass tournament and crappie fishing meccas, and the paradise washed away by their slowly rising waters — the Ozarks of my childhood in inalterable transition.

Lake Taneycomo on the White River, impounded by Powersite Dam in 1913, and the Lake of the Ozarks on the Osage River, completed with the construction of Bagnell Dam in 1931, were the Ozarks' major lakes in the first half of the 20th century.

The changes I recall began with the completion of Table Rock Dam upstream from Taneycomo in 1957. As I boy I saw my favorite fishing spot on Flat Creek disappear under the rising waters of the lake. I clearly remember fishing from a big, flat boulder in the stream and dropping my line into the swirling waters below. It was there I lost my first pocketknife, either kicked into the water or left lying on the rock. On our last return trip, I recall the rising waters on either side of the dirt road and watching a small brown snake slither through the water, flicking his forked, red tongue at me as he passed.

Years later I became friends with an old man who had worked at clearing timber for the lake basin. He left the Branson area for the Southwest in 1947 and did not return for 50 years. He was dismayed by the changes. When a beaming hotel clerk asked how he liked "our lovely Ozarks," he responded bluntly to the effect, "I don't. They've taken one of the most beautiful places on earth and ruined it."

Lake and tourism lovers would disagree, but many of us might not.

Nearer my home, Springfield City Utilities dammed the Sac River in 1954-55 to create Fellows Lake as a city drinking water reservoir upstream from smaller McDaniel Lake. Dad had grown up near there, hunting and fishing along the Sac as a youth. He knew the families that were displaced from ancestral farms and all the old roads closed by the lake. Before the lake completely filled, he took us fishing on the upper end. I recall following an old road to reach the water's edge—a road now deep below the lake.

Nearer my heart was the ravages caused by the creation of Lake Pomme de Terre with the building of a dam at Hermitage from 1957 to 1961. Though the dam was miles from my favorite stretch of the river near Fair Grove, the impact was catastrophic. The river where I learned to cast for smallmouth bass and big black perch with Dad's old bamboo flyrod was ruined. The spawning runs of huge largemouth came to a sudden end. In one season gamefish were replaced by hordes of small carp and fingerling bass. Never again would the Pomme de Terre near Fair Grove be the pristine stream I knew. It had become my "River of Used to Be."

Next to come in was Lake Stockton in 1969. Prior to completion of the dam on the Sac River hundreds of farmers were displaced — some from farmlands at Aldrich that were never actually flooded. The dam construction, however, did provide employment for some of my family, and the evacuation gave us some good new neighbors.

Most recent of the big lakes to be completed is also the state's largest—Truman Lake created in 1979 by a dam across the Osage at Warsaw. Known for years as the Kaysinger Bluff project, the massive impoundment reportedly became Truman after Stockton residents rejected the name.

Southwest Missouri's great lakes are undeniably valuable for their hydroelectric generation and flood control. Collectively, they have become the foundation of a multi-million-dollar tourism industry.

Yet, they have transformed the very landscape and character of the Ozarks into something our forebears would find alien and likely offensive. I frequent lakes because they are there. They have a character and appeal all their own. They are vital to our burgeoning outdoors and recreational industries. But I still like rivers. I grew up fishing and swimming in rivers, not lakes. Historically, rivers were highways into the heart of the Ozarks. Dams have turned them into raceways and parking lots for motorboats.

I suppose it will long be argued, when we look at the changes effected by these great dams, "Was it worth it?" Each of us has to answer for himself.

All I know for certain is, for better or worse, the Ozarks landscape of my childhood was not what I see today. But, I guess, neither am I.

Summer Silence Enwraps Old Farm

Jim Hamilton

I go down to our old farm often in summer to clip the grass around the house.

In many ways it looks the same as when Mom and Dad last lived there, but I no longer hear its heartbeat. The house stands as silent as stone, no fan humming in the bedroom window, no prattle of TV announcers sifting through the summer window screens, no voices lilting in the stagnant air.

I hear no hens cackling out behind the barn, no radio blaring country music in the milk parlor, neither the metered buzz of the electric fence charger. The rumble, squeaking, and groaning of Dad's old Ford pickup coming up the lane from the hayfield is conspicuously absent. Not a single cow or calf is heard bawling for attention. The well house pump is permanently stilled, and no hounds bark and yelp at the ends of their chains in the corner of the woods.

In my mind I can still see Dad sitting on a milk can by the fence, watching his small herd of beef cattle meander up their serpentine path from the pond to the barn—but only in my mind.

Today tall water hemlock envelops the barnlot, obscuring any vista from the barn to what remains of the pond.

Storm-wrinkled sheets of tin are beginning to come off the barn roof. Sunlight thrusts broad rays between the barn's weathered, gray oak boards. Its doors are wired shut, its hayloft a vast, empty cavern with floorboards a hazard to footsteps.

Dad's old Farmall tractor sits where it last died under an oak tree, sprouts growing up between its wheels. His brush mower is nearby against a walnut tree, overtaken by weeds. Mom and Dad's last vehicle—a worn out Ford van—sits behind the shed, a possum trail to it in the tall grass.

I remember places like this from my youth—old farmsteads abandoned during the Depression, after World War II or during the droughts of the early 1950s. I hunted rabbits around the old buildings or in their dewberry-choked Federal Land Bank fields.

But, this wasn't one of those places. This was home, the foundation of memories and experiences to last a lifetime. I helped fill the old barn with hay every summer, drew water to fill the stock tank in the barnyard, crawled under the business end of Jersey cows in the milking parlor. Not just the old house, but the whole farm—every field, tree, animal, brother and folks —cradled me like a child in a mother's arms. All that it was then combined to give life to who I am now.

But that was then.

Like the parents who nurtured me in youth, the old farm is no more, but for what lives in me.

Standing in the backyard now I see but shadows of what it once was, and I hear nothing. The heartbeat gone; its silence leaves me empty and hurting.

I can do nothing but turn away and walk back to my truck.

The Intersection of Time and Place

Mike Kaminski

When the light is green,
I turn left onto AR 180.

But when
It's red,
I watch
Ghosts cross paths.

By the apartments,
A fresh stage team
Readies for California.

In front of the auto shop,
A skinny boy breaks rank
To adjust his load.

Heading west
Past the gourmet pizza joint
Walks a mother with no tears left to shed.

Hold Fast

Mike Kaminski

Where the soil is thin,
Roots twist and cling

To anchor
Where they may;

Deepening cracks
Where they must;

Wedging themselves
Into baleful crags

To search
For dust and dew.

Cedar saplings
Tighten their grips

And prepare to enter
The breach.

Zero the Hero; or, From Factory Worker to Superhero in Sixty Days

Phillip Howerton

The orientation for my new job consisted of the supervisor handing me a hardhat, telling me I was required to wear white, and showing me how to operate the time clock. At 4:30 the next morning, March 4, 1984, I began my first day of work at Mid-America Dairymen in Lebanon, Missouri. Everything had fallen into place. Life lay before me as clear and structured as a long hallway with an exit at the far end. I was twenty-one and recently married, and I had landed one of the few union jobs in town.

The pay was good and the work simple. I was to unload and wash the bulk trucks that delivered raw milk from the local farms. Machines performed most of the work; electronic pumps transferred the milk from trucks to storage tanks, and the sprayers inserted in the manhole atop the trucks washed, rinsed, and sanitized the emptied tanks. Yet, it was wet and dirty work. The walls and floors had to be scrubbed daily, and dozens of pipes, hoses, and pumps had to be disassembled and washed by hand. Occasionally I would get a milk bath; that is, a milk line would vibrate apart at a connection, or a hose would burst and drench me with cold milk, and I would spend the rest of the day smelling like bad cheese. The trucks were always covered with dirt or mud or snow from the country roads, and when they crowded together in the unloading bay, I had to wedge between them to climb the ladders to the manholes. At the end of the day, I was soaked with water and milk and my white uniform was stained with dirt, mud, and butterfat.

And this work didn't stay done. The trucks were unloaded and washed each day only to return the next, and the work had no purpose beyond a paycheck. There were no honors or awards, no chance for promotion, no sense of accomplishment, and no marketable skills to learn. The only recognition I received during the fourteen years was a memo congratulating me for ten years of service—and this memo was delivered to me by being stapled to my paycheck eight months after the anniversary of my hiring. As do all hourly wage workers, I watched the clock, and the hours turned into days, and the days turned into years. One of my co-workers, a white-headed, taciturn man in his sixties, watched the clock for forty-one years before retiring.

I worked this job a couple of years before I started to feel sharp pangs of discontent. Some of my co-workers were like shadows as they performed the same tasks and mumbled the same complaints day upon day, season after season. I thought that there had to be more to life than working this repetitious, meaningless job. But for someone who had blown off high school and lived in a small town in the Ozarks, such a job was not easy to walk away from. It was one of the best-paying jobs in the area, and it offered life and health insurance, paid vacations, and overtime pay. Also, the work didn't follow me home. I could punch out and leave the job until the next day. And while I was on the clock, the job did not own me; it was a mindless task, and I disassociated myself from the work. Although my body was there, my mind was often elsewhere.

I started going to the public library on my lunch hour to browse through a variety of books, trying to find something that interested me. One day I noticed a poster on the library's bulletin board advertising correspondence courses offered by the University of Missouri-Columbia. I decided to enroll in *American History 101: Discovery to 1865*, and I told myself that if I did well in this course, I would enroll in others. It was not an easy decision. I had been out of high school for seven years, had a full-time job, and had started a small beef-farming operation. I wasn't sure that I had the time, money, or brains to do college—especially if I still did not know what I wanted to do with an education. However, going back to school in this manner would allow me to keep my job and take action to improve myself.

On June 30, 1998, I was laid off from this factory. I was thirty-six and recently divorced, and I believed that I had wasted approximately fourteen years working a dead-end job and nursing a dead-end marriage. The company was closing its Lebanon plant and had announced that production would be reduced and that approximately twenty people would be laid off each month until closure was achieved in mid-December. There were one hundred and fifteen production employees, and although I had more seniority than sixty-three of my co-workers, I volunteered to be the first to leave. Many of them had spent their entire working lives at the plant and were going to stay until the last possible moment ever hoping management might reverse its decision and gave them their livelihood back. After I left, twenty people received the proverbial pink slip in their paycheck at the end of each month, and the workers who remained would study the seniority list to calculate how much time they had left.

But I had jumped ship. It was sinking, and there were no lifeboats. All my coworkers were eventually forced to make a job change, but I had decided to make a life change. Besides taking correspondence courses, I had been attending evening college for nine years, often making a hundred-mile trip to campus at least twice each week after I got off work. I had earned a bachelor's in history and had almost completed a master's in education.

The school year was fast approaching, and I decided that I would take the first job in education that I could find. I was soon called in for an interview for a position as an assistant librarian at an elementary school. The superintendent told me that the pay was $10,000 for a nine-month contract and that the duties included "anything that needs to be done—whether it's working in the library, filling in for an absent teacher, or mopping up puke in the lunchroom." All of this sounded refreshing, and I eagerly signed on. I then volunteered to start a week early so that I could meet the librarian, learn the library's computer program, and help organize the stacks.

Although my primary duty was to scan and shelve books, I had plenty of time to work with the kids. I helped them find books, read to them, showed them how to do research on a computer, and helped them with their assignments. While on recess duty I pushed them on the swings and on the merry-go-rounds, played kick ball with the older boys, and turned one end of the long jump rope for the girls. On lunch duty I opened milk boxes, wiped up spills, and passed out "seconds" to kids who ate everything on their plate. On hallway duty I rubbed up black marks with the toe of my shoe, and, like Tom Sawyer and his whitewashing, I soon convinced several kids that wiping up black marks was fun. I was determined to be an incessant source of nonsense and laughter, and that was easy to accomplish. Compared to the vocational purgatory I had been in for fourteen years, I felt like I was in a theme park. Although my paycheck was one-third of what it had been, I was satisfied with the way I spent each day, and I looked forward to going to work every morning.

One day while I was at my computer scanning in a stack of returned books, Principal Smith, a heavyset, middle-aged man and a tenacious micro-manager, paraded in and stopped in front of my desk.

"Mr. Howerton. We didn't inform you of all of your duties when we interviewed you. We need you to be Zero," he said while seeming to focus all his attention upon toying with the small brass bell that we kept on the counter.

"And what is Zero?"

He paused as though suppressing a cough or chuckle, and then said in his principal tone, "Zero is a hero, and he visits the kindergarten classrooms on the number of school days ending with zero. The tenth day of school, the twentieth, and so on. The costume is in the supply room here in the library. You need to meet with the kindergarten teachers and schedule the day and time you will do this."

At the end of the day I rummaged through the dusty boxes in the library's supply room and found a large and silky one-piece blue suit, tailored much like a clown suit, with a zipper up the back and a large white zero on its chest, a red cape with another white zero, a two-piece mask made of newspaper and plaster of Paris painted a smooth, glossy blue with red wings on the ears—and a bicycle air horn. I then realized the principal's evil plan. Except for the custodians and a coach, he was the only male in the school. He may have viewed me as some sort of challenge to his authority, so he was attempting to humiliate me. Peter Parker was bitten by a radioactive spider to become Spiderman. Bruce Wayne witnessed the murder of his parents and then trained to become Batman. Superman came from a faraway world to become a hero on this planet of the yellow sun. I was a former Teamster simply wanting to shelve children's books in peace, but I was being forced to wear a clown suit.

*   *   *

While on lunch duty the next day, I slipped in beside the three kindergarten teachers at their table and interrupted their ravioli and chatter.

"I have a couple of questions. Who is Zero and what is he supposed to do?"

They immediately hushed and glanced questioningly at one another. Then Mrs. Wells, a thirty-year veteran, answered in a soft, coy voice as though she was answering a child's inquiry about human reproduction, "Why, Zero is from another world and *no one* knows who he is."

The other two giggled, and one added, "That's right. *No one* knows who Zero is."

Then Mrs. Wells asked seriously, "Why do you want to know?"

"Smith said that it is part of my job description."

They were thrilled. They said Zero was a lot of fun but that Smith had refused to do it the year before and that they had been forced to take turns.

As they explained it, Zero's duties were simple. He was to visit the kindergarten classrooms on zero days. The three kindergarten classes would gather in one classroom, and Zero would bring them a small edible treat shaped like a zero. Every snack he brought had served as something else in Zeroland and became edible only when Zero crossed into our world. The children had to discover what the snack had been in the other world before they were allowed to eat it. The main problem was that Zero had no mouth and could not speak, so the kids had to discover what the snack had been by playing twenty questions while Zero answered by honking the goose horn once for "No" and twice for "Yes."

I had to get back to lunch duty, for a group of kids was leaving and I needed to wipe up crumbs and spills. I told the teachers to let me know when they wanted me to make an appearance. They said, "This will be fun." "The kids will enjoy this so much." "This is sweet of you."

On my first visit as Zero the kids weren't certain what to make of the six-feet-four alien in a silky blue suit, with red cape and a blue head, and honking a bicycle horn. Some giggled, some sat very silent, some whimpered, but they soon figured out that Zero was a bearer of treats and that the peppermint Lifesavers had been roller skate wheels in Zeroland. An hour later, as the kindergarten class filed into the lunchroom, several of the kids stopped to tell me that Zero the Hero had visited and had honked his bicycle horn and had given them a piece of candy. They jabbered about Zero all during lunch, and some of them announced that they knew who Zero was, but they refused to share the secret. I realized then that Zero had potential.

With each of Zero's visits, the children became more receptive and Zero more expressive. Zero's personality seemed to blossom. He started doing simple math problems, with lots of zeroes, on the chalkboard. The teachers were surprised, for they had known Zero for several years and this was the first time he had ever written anything. Sometimes when he entered the classroom, he would ignore the teachers' attempted communications and would begin pointing out all the zeroes in the room. Zero found zeroes on the calendars, on the chalkboard, on the children's shirts, on the floor, and sometimes even a teacher's earrings were zeroes. He was fascinated with every zero, and since each one reminded him of his home, he would pause and place his hand over his heart when he found a new zero.

On one visit Zero was very tired because he had been flying all over the world visiting children, and he entered the room, not with his newly acquired trademark leap and pounding of his chest, but with dragging feet and bowed shoulders. He staggered across the room and dropped into the teacher's chair, propped his feet on her desk, and wiped his brow. The puzzled teacher asked Zero if he was tired. He honked his horn twice. To make Zero feel better, she then had the children sing a song that they had learned that morning. As they sang, Zero was re-energized, and leaped out of the chair honking his horn ready to celebrate zeroes.

Zero was always happy to share Zero Day with everyone, so after he had slipped into his costume in the kitchen supply room (the library closet had become too risky, for there was an absurd rumor circulating among the children that Zero was actually the assistant librarian, Mr. Howerton), Zero would chase the cooks around the kitchen honking his goose horn. He would then honk at Mr. Smith as he passed the principal's office, and then stop at the door of all the classrooms and honk his greetings, for most of the kids remembered him from their kindergarten days. Some of the teachers acted glad Zero stopped by to honk hello. His motto was "Honk until they smile." Some people required more honks than others. Zero would even sneak up behind people in the hallways and thrill them with his horn and then give them one of his edible zeroes. Mr. Smith mentioned to me that Zero might have to have his horn taken away, but I said that I had heard that Zero kept a backup horn in a secret zero place.

On a day just before Christmas vacation, Zero brought miniature doughnuts, and the kids quickly surmised that the doughnuts had been Christmas tree ornaments in Zeroland. But when the kids started eating the doughnuts, Zero was shocked. He started banging his head on the wall; he could not believe that the children would eat the ornaments from his Christmas tree. Zero protested by pacing back and forth, shaking his head, and throwing his arms in the air and stomping his feet—but this simply caused the kids to giggle and eat faster. Then Zero walked over to the classroom Christmas tree. He started rubbing his stomach and sniffing the ornaments. The kids continued to laugh at his antics until one perceptive little fellow shouted through a mouthful of doughnut, "He's gonna eat our decorations!" Some of the kids offered Zero the rest of their doughnuts, but he seemed determined (even though he didn't have a mouth) to taste a peppermint ring made of red and white construction paper. Mrs. Wells came to the rescue: "Children, this would be the perfect time to give Zero the present we made for him," and they shouted in agreement. They gave Zero a cardboard zero all of them had signed and had sprinkled with gold glitter. Zero held the glittering zero in his hand, wiped his eyes with his cape, and honked his horn again and again really fast.

The rumor that I was zero continued to grow. One day while I was on lunch duty, a table of kindergarteners informed me that they had proof that I was Zero. They had observed a beard under Zero's disguise and had noticed a red mark on my face that they believed to be caused by the mask. They also realized that Zero and I had never appeared in the same room together. I told them that Zero's feelings would be hurt if he knew that they thought he was a phony. To prove that I was not Zero, I promised I would come to their room to meet the hero the next time he visited. When I heard the horn honking on the next Zero Day, I hurried to the kindergarten room. There were several astonished small faces as Mrs. Wells introduced me to Zero—who appeared to be shorter and heavier (approximately the same size as Mr. Smith) than the last time I saw him. As I shook the hero's hand, I told him that the kids talked about him all of the time, that they were always excited about his visits, and that he deserved a raise. At lunch that day the previous doubters among the kindergartners did not hesitate to tell me that I wasn't Zero. One of them commented, "He's from another world." The others agreed.

Zero had fun one day out of ten, but I was having fun every day. Sure, everyone made a big fuss about Zero, but what did he ever do beside point at zeroes and honk that cursed horn? Although I wasn't as dynamic as Zero, I was doing okay for a mere earthling. I had memorized the library number of dozens of children, volunteered to work an extra hour of lunch duty each day, awed the boys by kicking the playground balls over the moon, spun the merry-go-round faster than a speeding bullet, and was dating a Lois Lane who taught at the school. I was also completing the last semester of a master's program and was teaching in an adult education classroom two evenings each week. More importantly, I had watched the seasons change, not by looking out the door of a truck bay, but, rather, by watching the hallway decorations change from a rainbow, to fall leaves, to jack-o-lanterns and black cats, to turkeys and pilgrims, and then to peppermint sticks and snowflakes. And instead of watching people grow old, I was watching people grow up, and I was watching them enjoy time rather than selling it. I visited the classrooms during holiday parties, celebrated with the kids when Mark McGuire broke the homerun record, and was on lunch duty the December day the kids stood and cheered when Mr. Smith announced that school was letting out early due to a possible ice storm.

Superheroes never need cash, but I was going broke. After taxes and insurance were deducted, my monthly paychecks were only about seven hundred dollars. This paid my rent, my utilities, and my truck payment. My earnings from my part-time job teaching adult basic education bought my gas and groceries. However, this part-time work unexpectedly led to a full-time teaching job. The salary of this new position exceeded what I had earned at the factory, and it included full benefits and career ladder—all within three blocks of my apartment. I had gone to college for ten years to be a teacher, and this position was obviously too good to turn down, but it wasn't a simple decision. As I considered the job change, I had to admit I was surviving, paying my bills, having fun, and had making a lot of little friends. But I had to think about the future, and I couldn't work for these low wages for the rest of my life. In January I turned in my two-week notice to Smith, and the school board graciously released me from my contract.

The last day I appeared as Zero was the 100th day of school, and since 100 has double zeroes, this was traditionally the last time that he visited each year. The kindergarten teachers arranged a party to celebrate the number 100 and to thank zero for his dedication to this much under-rated number. During the party the kids ate cake and drank Kool-Aid, and Zero had his photograph taken with each of them. Many gave him thank-you cards, several hugged him and told him good-bye, and some were crying. Zero was very quiet, for some things can't be said by honking a horn.

When the party was over, I hurried to the kitchen to get out of the suit for lunch duty. I pulled off the moistened mask, dried my eyes, and tried to rub away the red marks pressed into my face. I untied the cape and stepped out of the suit, stuffed Zero into his box, and carried the box to the library. Standing alone in the dusky quiet of the supply room, I took out the horn and honked it once. The room seemed to forbid such outbursts, so I gave the horn several hard squeezes. Its playful, garrulous tone seemed to unsettle the dust and startle the shadows, and I promised myself that I would take the tone of the horn with me. I then dropped the horn into the box, folded the four tattered flaps over one another, and placed the box on the shelf where I had found it only months before.

Book Reviews

***Fractals*. By Gerry Sloan. (River Oaks Press, 2021, Pp. 40)**

Reviewed by Phillip Howerton

Somewhere along the way in childhood I acquired a pen-sized microscope/telescope. This was one of my favorite toys. It was pocket-sized and practical, allowed me to look close and faraway, and lent perspective to mundane features of everyday life. *Fractals*, a chapbook of 36 poems by Fayetteville poet Gerry Sloan, has much in common with this long-lost gadget. This collection of terse verse is a compact granter of perspective, bringing both the near and distant into sharper focus to both my amusement and delight.

This little collection was produced by Andy Anders of River Oaks Press of Russellville, Arkansas, on an antique manual press using handset metal type and printed one sheet at a time. As I was told, this hand press was limited to 180 characters, and one of the poems used the full reserve of the letter *O*.

These 36 poems range in length from four words (including the title) to approximately sixty, and they deliver a wide range of tones, topics, and themes. Playful, witty, brooding, wry, and wise, these poems grant a sense of joining the poet on a hill to watch as the bustling, anxiety-laden, and narcissistic twenty-first century staggers past. Some topics are the pandemic, nature, human nature, inhumanity, racism, climate change, urban sprawl, and poetry—and the timeless topics of love, life, and death. You will enjoy reading many of these poems more than once, and there are several you will wish to share on social media or to memorize. Hmmm . . . when was the last time you were tempted to commit a poem to memory?

In its four lines, "In Absentia Muse" picks up the ancient topics of poetry and love, sprinkles on some self-effacing humor, and closes with a half line that is a superb lesson in form and function:

She says she respects and misses me too
though refuses to step out for a brew,

her messages growing more terse —
like my verse.

We are also given some purely charming love poems, such as
"Petite Chanson":

Inuits have many words for snow
and Arabs many words for sand,
but I've only one word for love
each time I hold your hand.

But, as shown in "But Will You Love Me Forever?" love
sometimes does not always run so smoothly:

When asked this timely question
and answering "I will try,"
I learned an important lesson:
most women prefer the lie.

The final irony stated in "3 Ironies" is a couplet that may lodge
itself in your thoughts and memory: "Prosthetic limbs proliferate /in
countries that we liberate."

One of the most amusing fractals, and one of the longest,
"Reciprocity," pushes readers through three stages of reaction. In the
first two lines, we may fall into the habitual solemnity we assume
when encountering the refrain of "Ashes to ashes and dust to dust,"
but we are made uncomfortable when this is immediately followed by
a reference to dirty old men. This ingrained response is then upended
by the tittering arrival of a lustful old woman:

Ashes to ashes
and dust to dust,
nothing more disgusting
than an old man's lust.
Unless, as I've come
to understand,

there's also a lustful
old woman on hand.

Every poem in this little collection is a jewel. Each one pauses and peeps through a crack in the fence of humanity and spies something worthy of reporting, whether it makes us cry, or laugh, or blush, or wish to spit in the eye of the peeper.

Only fifty copies were printed, so this is truly a limited edition and cannot be purchased through Amazon or Barnes and Noble or your "neighborhood" Walmart. If you contact Gerry, he might still have a copy. You can borrow mine, *but I will want it back.*

***Field Trip: Stories*. By James Fowler. (Cornerpost Press, 2022, Pp. 194)**

Reviewed by C. D. Albin

In a brief author's note at the beginning of his debut story collection *Field Trip*, James Fowler designates place as the soil "from which my characters rise and in which they become themselves." Yet unlike many authors who identify the notion of place as the source of their creativity, Fowler does not render, in the manner of Faulkner, a carefully mapped "postage stamp of native soil." Rather, his characters are frequent travelers who traverse not only interstates but also inner states, sojourners of the soul who learn that places of embarkation can be equally as significant as those of arrival, and that places visited along the journey can work a shaping magic as well.

Such lessons are particularly resonant for the young, who populate a high percentage of the stories in *Field Trip*. An apt example is Reed Warren, protagonist of the title story, who departs Biloxi, Mississippi, behind the wheel of his father's Avalon with no particular destination in mind. He simply heads north to escape Jubal Middle School and its "chief thug in residence" (1), Bryce Cobb, who has targeted newcomer Reed as a likely informant regarding Bryce's drug dealing and thievery. At least, this is the motivation Reed acknowledges for the first two hundred miles of his journey, during which he somehow avoids being recognized for what he is, "a twelve-year-old driving a stolen car" (1). Somewhere south of Little Rock, however, Reed joins forces with a moderately maternal ex-con named Raylene whose determination to re-unite with her daughters in north Missouri brings into focus Reed's deeper incentive for leaving Biloxi: "He just wanted to get away, maybe to make a statement that would have to be addressed on his return" (5). Just as Raylene seeks to mend family ruptures, so too does Reed, and their odd pairing forms a subtle paradigm for a number of stories in *Field Trip*.

"Undertow," the collection's haunting second selection, highlights one such pairing. In the story we follow the unnamed protagonist's deepening descent into depression after her second miscarriage. She has become "a housewife disinclined to leave the house, wondering at people who willingly, eagerly pack for Alaskan cruises and Machu Picchu" (20). She also must remain wary of newspapers, which can convey the travails of strangers, specifically the suffering of a young victim chased by other adolescents who pummel him with rocks and leave him tangled in a fence outside the city. An announcer on her car radio reports that this boy eventually succumbs to his injuries, news that leaves the woman unmoored as she cruises the asphalt arteries of her city until she crosses a causeway and arrives at a nearby island. There, among others who are physically isolated from the main population, she detects the wailing cries of a lost child. Coaxing him into her car, she decides "some people don't deserve children. If he were hers, he wouldn't be wandering the beach, at the mercy of strangers. . . . Two straying lives have converged" (30). The drama created by this convergence spotlights a meaningful motif that occurs frequently throughout *Field Trip*.

"Borders" offers yet another take on this plot pattern of cars, convergence, and travel. Unemployed teenager Mike, still living with his parents, feels hemmed in by the nature of life in small-town Arkansas, which he senses "could be a series of dead ends when it came to jobs and maybe even relations. That truth had lately come into focus for him now that high school was history" (32). The necessity of summer employment forces Mike into a job hunt, but the pickings prove dismally slim until he spies a flyer at the local market advertising a driving position "for $6/hr plus gas" (33). The ad is authored by one Jerzy Dubilas, a European writer touring the U.S. for a book project. Dubilas is personable enough to have impressed the market cashier as "not-from-these-parts-strange but short of creepy" (33), so Mike interviews for and gets the job, which ultimately offers enough enlightening experiences to help him peer beyond the boundaries of his small town and, indeed, Arkansas itself. As a consequence, "Borders" turns out to be one of the more hopeful stories in "Field Trip," with Mike broadening his personal range of possibilities even as his daily tours with Jerzy deepen his appreciation for the richness within, and without, Arkansas.

If "Borders" portrays a young man's initial awakening to life's larger potentials, "Second Growth," set in the Arkansas Ozarks, portrays an elderly man's warier, wearier embrace of new experience. Emmet Hollings, a recent widower, feels as if he has been "left to fend for himself in a house that [Phyllis] had always managed" (116), and his discomfiture only increases when the Rodriguezes, a Hispanic family who own the town's newest restaurant, rent the house next door. To his credit, Emmet does not indulge the blatant prejudice of some in his neighborhood (like one man who protests the growing Hispanic presence in the Ozarks by refusing to serve chicken at barbecues), nor does he join in the "old-guard talk" at Turk's Barber Shoppe, "talk that cross-stitched memories when it wasn't circling the wagons" (123). Yet Emmet is not without reservations regarding the new family next door. Early in the story his concerns read like a list of ethnic clichés, from the specter of declining property values and parties on the lawn to the scourge of drugs and crime. Yet the Rodriguezes, especially the children, are active and sometimes even gregarious, creating situations in which Emmet's gently harbored preconceptions are swept aside by the common humanity of flesh and blood people. As a result, his inward journeys turn out to be as substantial in their consequence as Reed Warren's journey from Biloxi to north Missouri, or Mike's explorations of the four corners of Arkansas. Emmet is even beginning to think "that he had it in him to surprise himself. Growing older, it seemed you could become both more set in your ways and less set in your attitudes" (125).

While Emmet Hollings is representative of the relatively few characters in this collection who stay put, at least physically, the inner growth to which he opens himself characterizes the most significant aspect of his fellow travelers within *Field Trip*. James Fowler is a traditional storyteller in this regard: he is careful to chart a character's significant decisions, those turning points in a person's life that occur in what we might call the deep interior, but which eventually manifest themselves in a character's conduct and values. There is certainly variety in Fowler's story structures, along with engaging humor and an often urbane narrative voice, but ultimately there is a notable spiritual aspect in this author's respect for the mystery of human quest and change. *Field Trip* may be Fowler's debut as an author of fiction, but it nevertheless proves to be a substantive addition to the literature of the mid-South region.

Wading Through Lethe. By Paulette Guerin. (FutureCycle Press, 2022, Pp. 84)

Reviewed by N. S. Boone

Paulette Guerin's first book is entitled *Wading Through Lethe*. The title is important, for it not only highlights the book's key themes of memory and loss, but it also indicates the function of the lyric in the volume. Lethe refers to the waters of oblivion. Plato, in Book 10 of *The Republic*, speaks of souls drinking of the waters of Lethe immediately before they are reincarnated and after they have spent 1,000 years in the afterlife. Lethe forces a forgetting of what has gone before, and, in Plato, clears the way for a new existence. But Guerin isn't drinking the waters of Lethe, she's wading in. It's as if the water itself is memory and Guerin's poems are an effort to find the salient pieces of the past in order to build a lost soul back together again.

Guerin's poems are lyrics, short lyrics. And one of the functions of the lyric is to stir up memory and desire. The book's first section is made up entirely of poems that come from the speaker's childhood — an Ozark Mountain childhood, with its obligatory churches, dirt roads, and small towns. Though you or I have never played in the same streams, watched boys jump off the same railway bridges into the same rivers, or heard the same worn-out church organs as Guerin's poems describe, we each are called back into the same child-like position—to remember what it was was like. But the lyric doesn't take one back to document or describe, it stirs memory by pointing to that salient aspect—that beautiful thing, that precious moment—perhaps not realized at the time. In fact, it may not have been realized at all until the poet brought it up within us:

At the Creek

"If only my memory were sharp again," she said,
sitting on a stump near the creek's edge.

I waded in the shallow cool, pants rolled, wet.
Her straw hat brimmed a shadow

over her face. The stones shimmered, each more
dazzling than the last.

We have been in a similar stream, shared a similar moment, but without the poet wading through Lethe to stir up these gem memories, those dazzling stones would never have resurfaced.

The book's first poem, "Gingko," is a kind of *ars poetica* for the volume:

Through the rain-thrash
and wind-sear,
the stems cling to each limb.

After the other trees
have metamorphosed
green to gold,
red to brown,
stems rattle in the dawn.

The ginkgo waits,
then lets go.
Brief burst
Of yellow.

The tight focus on the thing itself—the natural object—is apparent throughout the book, but most characteristic is the haiku-like effect of the final lines. Guerin's poems work this way—walking us through our own past, walking us through a scene we've been part of before, taking us to that Gingko tree we should have noticed, and perhaps did long ago. Then blasting us with the beauty and the irony wrapped so tightly together in the scene. The irony that never gets old, and which Guerin consistently picks out for us to notice, is the brevity of beauty. Something so perfect, so lovely, so fitting, so meaningful ought to last, and why not? In "Chicken Farm" she writes,

> On the banks of the river,
> a steering wheel dangles
>
> from a rope. While the boys
> swing and jump, she skips stones,
>
> noting the brief buoyancy
> before each is sucked back into the river.

Guerin's poems instruct us in how to handle the brief beauty—the moment when that stone rides the top of the water as if it were designed to do so—and the boys, like the stones, tossing themselves with abandon into the burying water. We see it again in "A Week Before She Died,":

> I ate one of her lemon bars
> Thinking nothing of holding
> Something so delicate
> It lost its shape in my hand.

How can we hold these beautifully brief gems? Only by wading through Lethe. Only through the lyricism of the poem. Guerin's best poems end with images that provide a striking sense of irony while not yielding to quick and easy interpretation. See "Y2K":

I turned fifteen and waiting for a beginning,
then an end. Mother stocked the cabinets with cans.
In the safe, she kept paper slips

with our names, dates, ink footprints.
On New Year's Eve, Grandma brought over
The gun she kept beneath her pillow.

We ate our lucky black-eyed peas
And watched the ball drop. The radio sat in the corner,
Batteries splayed around it like empty shells.

It's the perfect image to complete the scene. Empty shells, as in the empty promise of Y2K, of beginnings and endings, of something that will finally make a difference in the not-yet-filled life of a fifteen-year-old growing up in the Ozarks. What could fulfill a sense of yearning and adventure more than apocalypse? The empty shells recall, also, the empty bullet shells from the gun Grandma brought over and the violence teeming underneath the pieties and proprieties of this Ozark life, or, perhaps, under any life.

Lethe signals another facet of this volume—how Guerin exploits myth to amplify the meaning of salient pieces of memory, the precious moments. Mythical allusion is another way to press meaning beyond the bounds of imagistic, haiku-like poems. Penelope makes a couple of appearances, as do Sisyphus and Orpheus/Eurydice. Lot's wife (turned into a pillar of salt for looking back to Sodom in Genesis 19) is not explicitly mentioned, but her situation expresses a vital tension of what it means to wade through Lethe. In "Airport" the speaker disembarks from a plane into "a sepia world the color of things past" and she wonders "if glancing back would mean the end / of faith, the loss of promised things." The poems, of course, have all been acts of glancing back, of longing for beauty once held in hand. Glancing back to bring back up, to reconfigure, to build within one's soul a fountain of memory-filled waters. But glancing back is not looking forward, and this has been the critique of lyric nostalgia throughout the 20th century, beginning with the Modernists' critique of the Romantics.

Guerin knows her lyric jewel boxes have power—but is the power bewitching, or freeing?

In "The Little Mermaid Vacations in Florida" the speaker says, "If youth is possibility, adulthood is choice." The now human mermaid in the poem longs for her old life in the ocean: "Sometimes she forgets / how to walk, spending hours in the bath." In a hotel "she swims until the water is cold"; no longer able to hear her lover's talk, she can only hear the ocean where "There's just the water-whipped / rush of some large fish snagging a meal. / She's heard of people who swim / so far they can't go back." The poems all call us back to youthful possibility—the shining brilliance and beauty of youth. Adults want to swim back to it, and the poems could be siren calls to that end. But they can be otherwise, which is why Guerin provides critiques of nostalgia.

Poems must open possibility by providing choice. It's far too easy to be dazzled by jewelry in a box, to be turned into a pillar of salt listening to bewitching tales that call us back to lost beauty in melancholy tones. We pine for what's been lost, but we must choose what to do with it, knowing the consequences. Guerin gives us the choice, with a sort of classic Greek austerity, in "You can never go home again":

> but if you do,
>
> driving beneath the cocooned orbs
> of interstate lights,
>
> exiting toward a darkness
> where deer emerge like memories
>
> you hope to swerve and miss,
> resist
>
> thinking you could be anything
> beyond what this place expects,

that you won't open your mouth
for the bit.

Go back to youth, go back to this beauty of childhood possibility, but know that in going back you lose your freedom. In staying free, you can never go back.

The way out is the responsibility of the poet—to do more than look back. And Guerin realizes this even as she writes squarely in the mode of lyric nostalgia. The way out is deepening complexity—the tensions and ironies that can never be smoothed out and will never allow for easy rest in simple interpretation as in "Y2K," or "At the Coffee Shop" where Guerin's speaker says, "I'd give up the night, / but it's a given in this strange world / populated with imaginary friends, / where the self is not one but many." The way out also comes through pushing past lyric simplicities. Guerin's best poems work this way: stirring memory and desire, leading us by hand through Lethe, pulling out dazzling stones with which we construct fountains of memory within our souls.

1961 Ozark Breakaway: The Year McDonald County Seceded from Missouri. By Dwight Pogue. (Independently Published, 2021, Pp. 186)

Reviewed by Rocky Macy

Dwight Pogue's book, *1961 Ozark Breakaway: The Year McDonald County Seceded from Missouri*, travels sixty years back in time to reveal a unique episode in the history of the Ozarks. The book, as the title indicates, is about McDonald County, the southwest corner county of Missouri. But to a larger extent it is focused on the tourist town of Noel, located in the southwest quadrant of McDonald County, just three miles north of Arkansas and six or seven miles east of Oklahoma. Noel, which sits along the clear waters of the Elk River, was the tourist mecca of the county, and for many years it served as a weekend getaway for people from Kansas City and Tulsa and a vacation destination for much of the Midwest.

Dwight Pogue is a native of Noel, and in 1961, at the time this tale of political shenanigans and publicity stunts unfolds, he was sixteen, the son of the local newspaper publisher and right at the very center of the action. Sixty years later, after inheriting his father's printed materials and photos from that time, Pogue was the natural person to distill the events of that amazing summer onto the pages of a book.

The finished product is an homage to the community where he came of age, but, more importantly, it is also an accurate historical account of a special summer in the Ozarks. He chronicles events leading up to a county in semi-serious revolt against its state government, as well as the "secessionist" activities carried out that summer in an attempt to stir publicity—the lifeblood that would keep the tourists and their dollars flowing toward extreme southwest Missouri.

The story behind the events of that summer is this: In 1960 and 1961, McDonald County, and particularly the town of Noel, received a pair of grievous political insults from the government of Missouri. State Highway 71 was rerouted away from Noel without prior notice, a situation that literally left many confused on how to find the town. And then the state published a brochure about its tourist areas—and somehow managed to leave Noel out of that publication.

The town fathers complained to state officials in Jefferson City, and for the most part felt that their complaints were ignored. It was at that point that the topic of "secession" came up, and because 1961 was the 100th anniversary of the beginning of the Civil War, secession was a term that was understood and being talked about. A letter was introduced in the Missouri Legislature in which McDonald County withdrew from the state and expressed hope of forming a new state with the bordering counties of Benton (Arkansas) and Delaware (Oklahoma). Eventually the county went on its own and proclaimed itself to be "McDonald Territory." The ensuing publicity that summer was a windfall that more than made up for financial harm caused by the state's political machinations.

It was a summer featuring militia battles with residents of neighboring counties, a "land rush," antique cars, gun-toting hillbillies interfering with traffic, and all manner of well-intentioned mischief.

Newspaper editor and "Territory Press Secretary" Ralph Pogue, Dwight's dad, was keeping one foot close to the brake when he summed it up this way: "The McDonald County Secession fight should not be construed by anyone as a 'move of animosity' against the State of Missouri. If hatred and intent to get revenge enters into it, we will lose our battle."

For those seeking documented historical facts, they are in this book—aplenty. News articles of the times from a variety of sources—local, state, national, and even international—are included, as well as correspondence, maps, and hundreds of photos. And for those, like this reviewer, who was living in or around Noel at the time, Dwight Pogue's book offers a great place to relax and reminisce. Every page brings back memories right up and including the back cover—which features a couple of my dearest friends who have passed on.

And for those just looking for something fun to read—and perhaps to learn a little in the process—there is a lot of humor in Dwight Pogue's history of McDonald County's secessionist summer. Rivers Wylie was an older gentleman who drove his own car as a sort of private taxi in and around Noel. He was an early forerunner of an "Uber" person, and he was also quite a character. Dwight uses a quote from one of his father's newspaper columns in talking about Rivers Wylie, and his words give an indication as to some of the banter going around at the time: "Rivers Wylie recommends to the new Territorial Government the following tax program: No Retail Sales Tax, No Corporation Tax. No Income Tax. No Inheritance Tax. No Thumb Tax."

And though the Territory did issue its own postage stamps and wooden nickels, as far as I know it never collected any taxes from any source, thumb or otherwise!

1961 Ozark Breakaway: The Year McDonald County Seceded from Missouri by Dwight W. Pogue is intelligent, witty, and chock-full of facts about a most unusual summer in the Ozarks. Readers will enjoy and learn from this work, whether they had the good sense to have grown up in McDonald County or not!

Scattered Lights. **By Steve Wiegenstein. (Cornerpost Press 2020 Pp. 164)**

Reviewed by C. D. Albin

We have all seen them. Approaching a small town by night, we notice first the lights that spangle homes and businesses, and perhaps we project upon their luster the safety and comforts of community, the consoling promise of an outpost in the darkness. Yet in the new story collection *Scattered Lights*, author Steve Wiegenstein complicates casual assumptions about small town, rural life, his stories demonstrating how abruptly people can be stripped of sheltering securities only to find themselves "instantly at the edge of something" (101), they know not what.

Set primarily in Missouri's eastern Ozarks, Wiegenstein's stories often unfold in or near the aptly named town of Piedmont, roughly translated as "foothill." Given this geographic particular, *Scattered Lights* may be said to have a regional focus, but Wiegenstein shows no interest in exploiting the fetish of local color so habitually associated with Ozark fiction. Instead, he renders relatable characters caught up in individual conflicts and contradictions, and he probes their complexities at levels deep enough to fulfill Eudora Welty's dictum that "human life is fiction's only theme."

The character Larry is a prime example. Protagonist of both "The End of the World" and "Signs and Wonders," the two stories bookending *Scattered Lights*, Larry is someone about whom a lesser writer than Wiegenstein might be tempted to make mean-spirited fun. Fervently religious, Larry has left one fundamentalist church for another "in a dispute over Christian perfectionism, whether being born again could enable a person to become entirely free from sin" (5). Larry prefers the latter view, believing he has heard God declare "the soul is my perfect, glorious jewel" (5). Over the course of both stories, however, the risks Larry takes for the ideal of perfectionism grow more consequential, until by the end of the book he finds himself alone, listening not to the voice of God but to "the droning machinery of the exhausted world" (152). It is a testament to Wiegenstein's skill and compassion that we do not mock Larry's choices, but rather feel the depth of his weariness and despair.

Similarly, we identify with the bewildered angst of the teenaged Mark in "Weeds and Wildness." Mark has recently graduated from high school but "doesn't know what to do with himself." Despite his limited years, he has grown so weary of "the whole machinery of education" that he wants "to stop thinking for a while, to simply live, without the urgency of preparing himself for something yet to come" (14). What Mark has not yet learned, of course, is that something is always coming, in this case a request from the newly paroled father of a high school friend. The older man's appeal leaves Mark feeling as if "he had been maneuvered into something, but he didn't know what" (24). To his credit, he does not allow this dilemma to bury him deeper in his mental malaise, but rather summons the energy to seek direction, even when no clear path reveals itself to him. Fittingly, at the end of the story he crests a ridge and spots the "scattered lights" of Piedmont, which appear "seemingly random but somehow connected, if only he could see the pattern" (28). In realizing he must make the connections for himself, he begins his adult life.

A later blooming version of Mark is Chester Wilson, protagonist of the Wordsworth-echoing story "Late and Soon." Chester is another character who would prefer not to be disturbed by life's unpredictable demands or society's obsession with getting and spending. He is approaching middle-age and passes "too much of his time in bars" (111), habitually shifting his mind into "nobody-home-here mode, where it stayed most of the time out in the real world" (112). His withdrawal from that world is matched by his withdrawal from nature, even though he lives (courtesy of his father, the story implies) next to a golf course in Belle Prospect, which seems a combination of retirement community and time-share venture carved out of thickly forested Ozark landscape. Chester has built a cabin "in the scruffiest corner of his father's double lot" (112), yet he is so alienated from nature that he is one of the few Belle Prospect residents who does not sport a tan. Nor does he seem to have a job until his father arranges a position for him selling lots in Belle Prospect, an experience that ends abruptly and unsuccessfully. Presumably Chester is unsurprised by his failure, but the defeat moves him to the brink of a surprising choice, one that portends deeper commitment to the only person who won't enable his nobody-home-here avoidance.

Arguably the youngest protagonist in *Scattered Lights* is the one least inclined to shy away from reality. In "Magic Kids," fourteen-year-old Will stoically endures an unnamed but apparently terminal illness. The organization Magic Kids, which bears strong resemblance to the Make-A-Wish Foundation, sponsors Will and his family on a trip to Kansas City where he can experience a few brisk laps around a speedway with a prominent race car driver. The noisy setting of a speedway notwithstanding, "Magic Kids" turns out to be largely a story of silences, those awkward moments when people cross the boundaries of pretense and find themselves balancing, wordless, on the knife-edge of truth. One such moment occurs when Will, unable to sleep, wanders down to the lobby of the hotel where Magic Kids has booked the family a suite and begins a conversation with the desk clerk, only to learn that she has lost her only child to a heart defect. "He'd known this silence himself. Friends would come by, his friends, his parents' friends, and they would accidentally say something painful. And then the silence, or worse, the rush of apologies, more words trying to cover the earlier words, but never succeeding" (105). Perhaps because he is so young, or perhaps because he is tired of pretense, Will rarely tries to cover. The next day, when the race car driver asks him what he will do when he returns home, Will responds matter-of-factly: "I don't know. . . . Die, I guess" (108). His frank answer imposes silence on the small group gathered around him, bringing each to the edge of something rarely contemplated.

Good short stories lure readers into worlds of texture and consequence, where characters grapple with realities too often locked in shadowy back rooms of human consciousness. Likewise, good story collections adumbrate meaningful associations between individual stories, coaxing readers to puzzle out the links much as Mark from "Weeds and Wildness" does when he seeks a pattern in the scattered lights of Piedmont. Steve Wiegenstein's *Scattered Lights* is such a collection, good in quality and in spirit. To read it is to find reward.

***Tornado Drill.* By Dave Malone. (Kelsay Books, 2022, Pp. 100)**

Review by Paulette Guerin

Dave Malone's seventh poetry collection *Tornado Drill* offers a landscape of everyday people working and living, of sunrises and sunsets, of old lovers, of wrens who "drown the sky in flight." With grace, but without sentimentality, Malone's poems follow these currents through the Midwest.

The collection is divided into five sections, *Growing Up, Town, Memory, Quarantine,* and *Finning the Deep.* The opening poem, "Tornado Drill" tells us about the speaker we follow in many of these poems: while his classmates huddle beneath their desks, he "scramble[s] to the glass" for a better view as "the earth roars and the sky paints / the classroom windows cocoa." The excitement of seeing outweighs the risk, or maybe he doesn't yet fully understand the consequences of recklessness, a truth he will learn in later poems.

The tornado makes other appearances. In "Confetti" we are told the widow at the recycling plant lost her husband to it the year before, and the phrase "after the tornado" frames another poem. We see indirectly the aftermath of an event people will talk about for years to come, possibly the most noteworthy thing to happen in a long time. Even when there is no tornado present, the clouds on the horizon may do damage or press a person in. One exception: while in quarantine a woman prepares her cheap backyard pool and chases off a storm, a wonderful moment of imagined power during a helpless time.

The poems in *Tornado Drill* pay close attention to sound and are a pleasure to read aloud: "Dust motes float and sparkle / above the tongues of our sneakers"; "Blue heron babies / small as saplings / flap up from the shore / and crash into cedars / on the bluff"; or this excerpt from "The Nuisance of Nouns":

> "The katydids and cicadas
> whir and scratch
> while the bass
> fin the deep.
> If you stay long enough,

there's talk
between you and them."

Malone's poems remind us of a youth spent outdoors, whether it's burying a beloved dog or hitchhiking to a lake forty miles away. In "Recalling Light" Malone contrasts the education one receives indoors in church versus outdoors, presenting outside as a child's true place of learning and religion: "I remember now / the gospel the instructor ignored— / how the cypress floor danced / with golden dust in its hair." As the speaker approaches adolescence, priorities shift. "The 9:15 to Memphis" opens with one of the many characters populating the manuscript, the neighbor who gave tomatoes to the kids to take home—which they instead "used for fastball practice"—but ends with the gardener's daughters, signaling a new preoccupation.

The townsfolk are at times part of the background, at others, sharply in focus. We meet the schoolteacher putting her laundry out to dry, the pregnant mother trying to rest in a hammock, the neighbor running her leaf blower while the speaker tries to meditate. There are also portraits of elementary school classmates, a cashier who walks to the river on her break, and a hairdresser with moonlight pouring from her eyes.

In "Middle School Swimming Lessons" we open with an "Ozark summer sky" that "rippled like worn denim" and the teenage instructor inside calling the swimmers with "a shrill whistle [that] pierced ear to elbow." Halfway, the poem pivots and admits, "there's not much to remember," an understatement but also a truth about fragments of memory. The poem ends in a dreamlike setting, underwater, "inside the impenetrable boggish fog / then the thud and fade of heartbeat." Also dreamlike in its reverie is "Youth Camp," in which the boys leave their tent "to hunt / the early morning light," but instead find "a lonesome doe / in the dark woods," "the hint of presence, / of blueness, / of breath." They go deeper into the woods, their footing unsure, finding "a cemetery of moss," the boys' eyes "blind like the dead" as they feel their way forward to higher ground. The hill shakes "with the stomp of the unknown," perhaps the doe flitting away, but with echoes of resurrection or right of passage.

Soon, the speaker is old enough and has seen enough to know loss—and be wary of it. For example, at fifteen he finally has a seat at the table to play Pitch, teamed up with an uncle whose missing fingers remind the speaker that some loss is forever visible. The poem ends with him "scared / to bid five tricks to win the game, / fearful of that hand, of what [he] might lose." Other people in the collection face loss as well. The mother in "Easter Egg Hunt" waits for her soon-to-be eighteen-year-old to collect the chocolate she's hidden in the yard, but as "the nearing storm wails, she knows / he won't make it home in time."

Later poems recollect romantic relationships, some good, some bad. We meet a lover who loses the rent money at video poker, another who helps the speaker toss their mattress in the dumpster. In "We Don't Check Our Phones," a couple escapes both the virus and cabin fever by unplugging and heading to the woods. It could be idyllic, but they quibble over flower names, a very human thing to do—a modern Adam and Eve having a spat as they try to reenter Paradise. In "Pencil a Venn Diagram with an Intersection of Sets," we learn about the separate lives of two people and where, after meeting, they begin to overlap: their discovery that

> "they don't like to talk much on Sundays
> and love the final light of day weaving the woods
>
> in ribbons of color, the smell of upturned earth
> on the farm in March, the pluck of the two-lane
>
> that leads into town and how it swoops like a skirt,
> how the truck tires rattle and boom like horns."

If many of the middle poems are character portraits, the final section spends more time in nature. We see, too, Taoist influences with references to awareness and consciousness. A return to a cave, an abandoned farmhouse, the memory of laundry once hanging on the line. A place where "even the cicadas lash out in rhythm." Or the gift of a tree root tripping the speaker so that he becomes "Awake!"

Without being didactic, these poems show what we can learn through close observation of the natural world.

In *Tornado Drill* Malone privileges normal people living everyday lives. Place is important, and people are important to a place. Malone's poems also look for moments the Romantic poet William Wordsworth would say were "bathed in celestial light." Or as Malone would put it, "the air is cold and crisp with wonder, / and you can't be dead." If in *Tornado Drill* there is destruction, it is counterbalanced with the lives people have built and rebuilt, and the resilience of moving forward.

Rube Tube: CBS and Rural Comedy in the Sixties. By Sara K. Eskridge. (University of Missouri Press, 2018, Pp. 242)

Reviewed by Tim G. Nutt

Some of the most fondly remembered television shows in syndication today are the rural comedies which aired on the Columbia Broadcasting System (CBS) during the mid-late 1960s. In *Rube Tube: CBS and Rural Comedy in the Sixties*, Sara K. Eskridge examines the popularity of these shows, the disconnect between the shows amid shifting social changes, and their abrupt cancellation.

Beginning in 1960 with the premiere of *The Andy Griffith Show*, the comedic lives of residents of rural communities of Hooterville, Mayberry, and Kornfield Kounty, as well as the fish-out-of-water story of the Ozarks "hillbillies" in Beverly Hills, became staples of the CBS television lineup. This slew of country-oriented shows in the 1960s was a drastic shift from the programming that dominated CBS's lineup in the 1950s, which centered around shows set in urban or suburban locales.

What was the reasoning behind such a sharp pivot? Eskridge adeptly explains that CBS executives in the 1950s focused programming on more thought-provoking, erudite, and even diverse casting and topics. *I Love Lucy*, which aired on CBS from 1951-1957, featured real-life couple Lucille Ball and Desi Arnaz. Arnaz was one of the first Latino actors to headline a network television show and portray a successful career man. While Black representation was present on CBS in the 1950s—with shows such as *Amos 'n' Andy*—stereotypes were heavily utilized in plots and characters. Even with these stereotypes, executives worried about finding sponsors for shows featuring Black actors, as well as offending Southern viewers.

Although slavery had been abolished for nearly a century, Blacks in the southern United States still found themselves denied rights through segregation policies and Jim Crow laws. Beginning in 1954 with the U. S. Supreme Court decision *Brown vs. Board of Education of Topeka*, laws segregating Blacks from white society were challenged. In 1957, the integration of Central High School in Little Rock by nine Black students resulted in a stand-off between Arkansas Governor Orval Faubus and the Federal Government. Faubus' defiance of an integration order was broadcast around the country. The era of Civil Rights had arrived and, as Eskridge writes, CBS executives erased much, if not all, of the earlier diversity in favor of shows that were "inoffensive yet entertaining to a broad swath of the population. . . ." (9).

The shift in programming resulted in a rash of rural-centered, farcical shows written to display the antics of hillbillies and other rural folks in all their perceived uncouth, simple, and folksy ways. While these new programs played to the stereotypes associated with rural or hill folk, they were meant to connect Southern audiences with the television characters and to be inoffensive to sponsors and to the audience. Most of these new shows rarely featured a Black or Latino character. As Eskridge notes, these programs "served as a peacemaker between CBS and the public" (9). They also became money-makers for the network, and many are considered classics and remain on the air nearly sixty years after their first airings.

The Andy Griffith Show led the transformation of CBS from the "Communist Broadcasting System" (which many called it because of its diversity and liberal bent in the 1950s) to the "Country Broad-casting System" (93). A list of the "rural comedies" selected by CBS executives in the 1960s can still be found on the television dial today, including *The Andy Griffith Show, Petticoat Junction, The Beverly Hillbillies, Green Acres,* and *Hee Haw.* All of these shows relied on comedy resulting from misunderstandings, cultural differences, sight gags, or physical pratfalls. *Hee Haw,* probably the most ridiculous in this grouping, was built on cringe-worthy jokes and hokey skits, but it also gave a venue to some of America's biggest country stars.

CBS found success in this programming because the shows were popular throughout the country, not just in the South. These shows ruled the Nielson ratings because of their universal popularity. Eskridge proposes that the popularity of this programming, especially outside of the South, was because it made "viewers feel better about themselves" (141). The escapist element of the shows also triggered a sense of nostalgia among viewers.

Despite the high profitability and popularity of the shows, those still on the air in 1971 were abruptly cancelled. CBS executives in the 1970s purged the schedule of the rural comedies, greenlighting edgier, more diverse, and socially conscious shows, such as *All in the Family*, *The Jeffersons*, and *The Mary Tyler Moore Show*.

Eskridge provides an excellent, insightful look into 1960s society through the screen of the television set. With research conducted at prestigious archives like Performing Arts Special Collections at UCLA, National Archives, and the Academy of Television Arts and Sciences, Eskridge has made a significant contribution to our knowledge of media history, particularly in the "rural" era of CBS. I highly recommend this book.

LOST & FOUND: *Poems Found All Around*. By Greg Zeck. (Dead White Man Press, 2021, Pp. 140)

Reviewed by Gerry Sloan

The poems encountered in *Lost & Found* remind us that poetry exists right under our noses and is omnipresent if we only tune in to its frequency. Some imply a particular attitude, a tilted way of observing the world in all of its stunning plenitude. The poet is not just the creator but also the curator who places a frame around a text or experience to draw our attention, often resulting in irony or potential epiphany, an instance announced in the opening epigram:

Frame
By way of epigraph

I put a frame around it
so I can say I found it,
so I can say it's yours and mine
for this brief space of time.

Recontextualization has played a prominent role in post-modern art, but no verbal artist I know has taken it to this extreme. Of course, T. S. Eliot's *The Waste Land* (1922) was peppered with quotes, but I have never seen an entire collection based on this procedure. At times the ghosts of Robert Creeley and John Berryman, as well as deceased family members, peer over Zeck's (and consequently *our*) shoulder, but they produce a welcome species of haunting. I can think of nothing quite like it in the body of American literature. John Cage is probably smiling somewhere at anyone daring to dance this intimately with the products of chance.

In a three-page foreword, Zeck reveals his inspirations and modus operandi, the poems contained in eight loose groupings with sub-headings like: "Capitalism and Its Discontents," "News of the Day," "When We Have Fears that We May Cease to Be," and "Messages from the Living & the Dead," followed by copious Endnotes to guide readers through this language museum. From the foreword: "Words are all around us. They're the cultural and biological soup in which we live and swim." Be sure to bring a flotation device so you can linger in such rich broth.

Section 7 ("When We Have Fears") is mostly re-framing the words of Soviet author and Nobel Prize winner Svetlana Alexievich. They might serve as a welcome corrective to our current anti-Russian hysteria. Then he brings us closer to home in a sassy prose-poem called "Things to Do in Evening Shade, Arkansas," which ends: "So how about a place to pitch my tent in Evening Shade? Just a campground or backyard innocent of guile or suspicion of strangers that I might try out, like a final resting place, trying if the ground is comfy, rocky, or just right, somewhere, anywhere for a son of man to lay his head," echoing Eliot's opening of *The Waste Land* : "Son of man,

/ You cannot say, or guess, for you know only / A heap of broken images. . . ."

This book is a tourist guide through the broken images of current culture. Some of the poems play with typography (e. g. "Poem in Form of a To-Do List," "Dung Beetle," "Base Jump," and "The Void"). One of the final (humorous) poems is how (not) to write your own obituary ("before your heirs [*bleep*] it up"). Some poems are ironic, verging on sarcasm. Some even find room for tenderness, as in the elegies for siblings. Zeck takes an etymologist's delight in digging around in the roots of words, then riffing like a jazz musician or free-style rapper on what he has found. And lost. And helped us all to find again.

Oklahoma Odyssey. By John Mort. (University of Nebraska Press, 2022, Pp. 310)

Reviewed by C. D. Albin

It is doubtful many participants in the 1893 land run on the Cherokee Outlet—an area constituting a sizeable portion of today's northern Oklahoma—considered themselves comparable to characters in the epic Greek poem *The Odyssey*. The pell-mell pace of the event itself, much less the desperate, hurley-burley days of preparation along the Kansas border, likely displaced thoughts of literature, art, or culture, even for participants inclined toward such contemplations. Yet author John Mort, who recently received the Richard Sullivan Prize for *Down Along the Piney: Ozarks Stories*, has chosen the ultra-raucous 1893 land run as the historical setting for *Oklahoma Odyssey*, a novel in which principal characters are devotees of Homeric narrative. The result is a novel that proves simultaneously brisk and deliberate, action-packed and contemplative. Mort achieves such balance by credibly characterizing three young, large-souled adventurers linked not only by friendship, but also by a compulsion to maintain moral identity rather than give in to pressures of personal and historical circumstance.

Oklahoma Odyssey's primary protagonist is Ulysses (aka Euly) Kreider, a sober young Mennonite whose father's murder sparks the dramatic action of the novel. Despite the exploits of Euly's literary namesake, and despite his admiration for *The Odyssey* itself, Euly shows few early signs of becoming an adventurer. Rather, in the opening scene, a grousing Euly stews while departing Jericho Springs, Kansas, resentful that he has been shortchanged by a local merchant in whose eyes he is "just an ignorant Mennonite kid" (3). Yet Euly's business acumen is advanced beyond his years, honed by a studious appreciation for his father's mantra: "the only way to make a profit in this world, Ulysses, is to offer a man something he can't do without" (3). As a result, Euly's commercial endeavors maintain ongoing relevance in the narrative, ultimately proving responsible for his presence in the Cherokee Outlet at the culmination of the novel.

Those business interests are no more relevant than Euly's religious commitments, however. By the novel's second chapter, Euly has announced that he "will not seek revenge" (11) on Eddie Mole, the outlaw who shot, then robbed, his father. With such a declaration, Euly joins the scant ranks of protagonists in American literature, like Bayard Sartoris in William Faulkner's "An Odor of Verbena" and Sam Simoneaux in Tim Gautreaux's *The Missing*, who reject their society's call for violence as the most heroic response to the murder of family members. Moreover, given that Mort ostensibly positions *Oklahoma Odyssey* within the Western genre, his choice to explore nonviolence as a response to injustice invests the novel with additional artistic and ethical significance.

While Euly maintains a commitment to pacifism regarding his father's murder, the farm laborer John Baxter (who embraces his own Osage heritage by choosing the name Johnny Heart of Oak) is less swayed, initially at least, by notions of nonviolence. A survivor of boarding school, where "whites belittled his culture, suppressed his religion, tried to replace his language" (86), Johnny is initially motivated by a different ethic than that of his best friend Euly: "Eddie Mole ought to be killed by. . . Ulysses Kreider. Johnny should only count coup" (65). Yet killing Mole would put a substantial reward into Johnny's hands and provide ample funds for him to marry Euly's half sister Kate. Thus conflicted, Johnny sets off into the Cherokee Outlet in search of Mole. The upshot is that at the end of the search, Johnny finds not only the murderer, but also a clearer, more definitive understanding of himself. To Mort's credit, that understanding accommodates nuances from both the Caucasian and Indigenous aspects of Johnny's cultural experiences, eventually enabling him to chant, "I am John Baxter, John Baxter. I am a rich man" (121).

The woman whom John Baxter loves, Kate Kreider, is arguably more conflicted regarding identity than any other character in the novel. Raised to think of Euly's father Barney as her uncle, she discovers only after the man's murder that he was her father too. Equally perplexing, Kate knows nothing about her mother, although a dark complexion, dark eyes, and curly hair lead one friend to declare Kate a "Negress" (136), while others conjecture that she possesses native heredity. Were she to marry John Baxter/Johnny Heart of Oak, racial identity would present still more maddening complications. In Missouri, a marriage between an Osage man and a woman passing as white would not be legal, but, as Johnny tells her, "We are legal in Kansas. In Oklahoma, they have no law" (161). Add to all this Kate's frustrations regarding the societal limitations placed on her gender. "What, in the spring of 1893," she asks herself, "could a woman be" (129)? Ultimately, she takes transformative assurance from Johnny's declaration "You are Osage" (162), a proclamation that carries the moral authority of acceptance if not the proof of racial identity.

Like his sister Kate, Euly Kreider undergoes a transformation as well, eventually growing into the noble patterns of behavior suggested by the nickname "Little Hero" that Johnny Heart of Oak coined for him long ago. And, while injustices and betrayals are visited upon Euly by strangers and family alike, at the end of the novel he proves able to deliver a live, breathing Eddie Mole to Kansas authorities, who are happy to proclaim Euly "a big hero" (306). Having accomplished such a feat without compromising his religious beliefs, he is satisfied to return home to the woman he regards as "his faithful Penelope" (308). That not-so-subtle detail, echoing as it does the return of Homer's Ulysses, seems a final reminder on Mort's part that *Oklahoma Odyssey* can be read in the context of both historic drama and classic literature. Additionally, it reminds us that our conflicts with integrity and identity remain pertinent no matter the time or place in which we reside. Everyone makes choices, the book seems to say, and they mark us as little heroes or not.

Queen of the Hillbillies: Writings of May Kennedy McCord. **By May Kennedy McCord. Edited by Patti McCord and Kristene Sutliff. (University of Arkansas Press, 2022, Pp. 336)**

Reviewed by Leigh Adams

May Kennedy McCord may never have written her own book, but her granddaughter Patti McCord and retired Missouri State University professor Kristene Sutliff have edited a collection of her work drawn from both her published and unpublished writings titled *Queen of the Hillbillies: Writings of May Kennedy McCord.*

Published by the University of Arkansas Press as part of its Chronicles of the Ozarks series, the book is broken into subject categories that include geography, history, culture, customs, music, folklore, and flora and fauna. The pieces include material from McCord's columns for two different Springfield, Missouri, newspapers, her private papers, and KWTO's magazine *Dial*. The material covers the 1930s through the 1960s.

McCord's writing is lively, and as often as not, she seems to include the voices of the many readers from all over the Ozarks who wrote to her to comment on her columns or to add to or correct them. Many times, she wants to set the record straight for readers about the Ozarks' people, language, and culture, and she generously shares what she learns from those loyal readers.

Though McCord wasn't a trained folklorist, a lot of what she collected and published would easily fall into that category. Born in Carthage, Missouri, and raised in Galena, McCord has a clear love for the land, the people, and their stories and music, and she often wrote and spoke about them as well as welcomed more information. In one example from the chapter on death and burial, McCord writes about feather crowns, pillow feathers that wind themselves together so "that a crown would form in the pillow of a dying person, especially if the person had lived a good and saintly life" (124). The editors then follow this piece with several examples of stories on the subject sent in by her readers over the next seven months. Certainly, McCord's columns were participatory long before the days of social media.

The best part of reading this book is McCord's voice. Her turns of phrase are often fascinating and funny, and she has a keen eye for how to skewer particular types of people. Noting of one gentleman, "He wasn't worth the powder and lead to blow him into the next dispensation, but he could sit longer, lie harder, and spit farther than any yokel who ever wore shoe leather. . . " (55).

In a piece from her personal papers, she begins a story about an Ozarks politician by noting of politicians in general, "If I were a politician, I wouldn't have any trouble about a speech. A politician always has just one, and when you've heard it, you're all washed up with him. He points with pride and he views with alarm. He consumes a lot of water from a pitcher during his speech. It looks important" (104). She ends the piece by noting of the unnamed politician, "He was a good chap. He didn't have much book learnin', and his diploma wasn't made of sheepskin and tied with a ribbon, but it was made of rugged honesty. He wove his own philosophy from the solitude of his own mountains, and you know, sometimes there spring up men like that who shake nations" (105).

One of the more entertaining pieces appears in the chapter titled "The Ozarks Country." In it, McCord "reviews" a Thomas Hart Benton's painting *Ozark Musicians*. The piece begins, "When a Hillbilly tries to go 'arty' it's time something should be done. It was raining like pouring buttermilk out of a jug, but little did that matter—I had to see what it was all about. 'Art for Art's sake, you know'"(42). What follows is a thorough roast of the artist and his painting, which she deems a caricature. She is generous enough to note, though, that as she travels to other places, she fears she might fall into that same trap despite her good intentions.

And that's a good part of the charm of *Queen of the Hillbillies*. Not only does she not hold back her opinions on all kinds of subjects, but McCord's writing gives readers the delight of phrases like the one above analogizing rain with pouring buttermilk as well as a look into the ongoing work of showing and preserving what is real and good about the Ozarks and its people.

Contributors

Leigh Adams isn't from around here, but she's lived two thirds of her life in the Southern Missouri Ozarks and shares a deep affinity for its land and people. An associate professor of English at Missouri State University-West Plains, she worked with C. D. Albin to produce *Elder Mountain: A Journal of Ozarks Studies* as its assistant editor. She is a co-founder of the Ozarks Studies Symposium at MSU-WP and is a founding member and officer of the Ozarks Studies Association.

C. D. Albin is a professor of English at Missouri State University–West Plains. In 2009, he became the founding editor of *Elder Mountain: A Journal of Ozarks Studies*. His fiction, poetry, essays, and reviews have appeared in a number of publications, including *Arkansas Review*, *Big Muddy*, *Cape Rock*, *Cave Region Review*, *Georgia Review*, *Harvard Review*, *Natural Bridge*, *Philological Review*, and *Style*. Ten of his short stories were collected in *Hard Toward Home*, published by Press 53 in 2016, a collection for which Albin received the Missouri Author Award from the Missouri Library Association in 2017. His poetry collection, *Axe, Fire, Mule*, was published by Golden Antelope Press in 2018. He is currently compiling and editing *Storied Hills: Contemporary Ozarks Fiction*.

Wilson Allen is a sometimes poet, a full-time dog lover, and an avid hoarder of pork n' beans. He plans to retire from his day job the moment he turns 62 and then read himself into oblivion. His dissertation was once used as a door stop by his alma mater for two months, and both of his books can occasionally be found in discount bins at used bookstores—the ones they don't bother rolling inside during summer.

Michelle Collins Anderson grew up on a registered Angus cattle farm outside of West Plains, Missouri — a place and a way of life that has shaped her writing. She holds a journalism degree from the University of Missouri and an MFA from Warren Wilson College. Her stories have appeared in *Nimrod International Journal*, *Midwestern Gothic*, *bosque*, *Literal Latté*, *The Lascaux Review*, *Pooled Ink*, and *Literary Mama*.

Michelle lives in Liberty, Missouri, with her husband and three children. She is currently seeking representation/publication for her first novel, *The Flower Sisters*, based on the West Plains dance hall explosion of 1928.

N. S. Boone's academic essays range from scholarship on D. H. Lawrence, Mark Twain, Nathaniel Hawthorne, and E. A. Poe, to Homer, the Book of Revelation, and the seventeenth-century vegetarian Thomas Tryon. He's also written on the poetry of William Carlos Williams, Jorie Graham, Rita Dove, Mark Strand, and more. He's published poems in *Streetlight Magazine*, *Cave Region Review*, *St. Austin Review*, *Georgetown Review*, and elsewhere. He likes to fish and preach.

Marcus Cafagña took up writing poetry after he stopped playing the violin. He is the author of three books, *The Broken World*, selected by Yusef Komunyakaa for The National Poetry Series, *Roman Fever*, and the forthcoming *All The Rage In The Afterlife This Season*. His poems have appeared in *Cave Region Review*, *Chiron Review*, *Crazyhorse*, *Elder Mountain: Journal of Ozarks Studies*, *Poetry*, the *Southern Review*, *Witness*, *Yonder Mountain: An Ozarks Anthology*, among other journals and anthologies. He teaches poetry writing and poetry as literature at Missouri State University in Springfield. He was born in Michigan and raised by parents of Italian and Spanish heritage. He moved from Philadelphia to the Ozarks twenty-three years ago.

Jenny Crews was born in Joplin, Missouri, and moved to Springfield where she has lived since she was twelve (except for a one-year stint in Austin, Texas, back in the 80s). In 2017 she retired from Missouri State University where she served as Director of Prospect Management and Research in the Office of Development and Alumni Relations. She is also a Missouri State University Alumna, having received a BA in English/Creative Writing in 1996.

Cathie English teaches undergraduate and graduate English education courses at Missouri State University after a twenty-two-year career in secondary English education. Her research focuses upon place conscious education with an emphasis in community literacy, teacher leadership, and composition theory and practice. Her work can be found in *English Journal, Journal of Literacy Innovation,* "Work Ethnographies" in *Writing Suburban Citizenship: Place-Conscious Education and the Conundrum of Suburbia* at Syracuse University Press, and "A Forever Student Navigating Higher Education: Reflections of a First-Generation Scholar" in *Teacher Reflections on Transitioning from K-12 to Higher Education* at IGI Global.

Paulette Guerin is the author of the poetry collection *Wading Through Lethe* and the chapbook *Polishing Silver*. She is a graduate of the MFA program at the University of Florida. She lives in Arkansas and teaches writing, literature, and film. Her poetry has appeared in *Best New Poets, ep;phany, Contemporary Verse 2,* and others. Her website is pauletteguerin.com.

Jim Hamilton was brought up on a small dairy farm in southern Dallas County near Elkland, Missouri. In 1970-71 he was editor of the Southwest Missouri State College *Standard,* and from 1971 to 1974 he served his country as a U.S. Air Force journalist and base newspaper editor. After earning a BA in writing at Southwest Missouri State University in 1974, he worked as a news editor at the *Bolivar Herald-Free Press*. In 1977 he returned to SMSU for a master's degree and then began a 24-year stint as editor and publisher of the *Buffalo Reflex*. For more than forty years, Hamilton has produced weekly editorial columns, and collections of these were published as *The River of Used To Be* (1994) and *Ozarks RFD: Selected Essays* (2020). *Ozarks RFD* received the 2020 Nonfiction Book Award from the Ozarks Writers League. Ostensibly retired since 2015, Hamilton and his wife live on a small acreage outside Buffalo with two steers, 20 chickens, and one dog. Inducted into the Regional Media Hall of Fame and the Missouri Press Association Hall of Fame in 2016, Hamilton continues to pen weekly columns for a half-dozen Ozarks newspapers.

John J. Han, Ph.D., is Professor of English & Creative Writing and Chair of the Humanities Division at Missouri Baptist University. He is the author, editor, co-editor, or translator of twenty-eight books, including *Worlds Gone Awry: Essays on Dystopian Fiction* (McFarland, 2018), *The Final Crossing: Death and Dying in Literature* (Peter Lang, 2015), and *Wise Blood: A Re-Consideration* (Rodopi, 2011). His peer-reviewed essays on Ozarks literature have appeared in *POMPA: Publications of the Mississippi Philological Association*, *Philological Review*, *Intégrité: A Faith and Learning Journal*, and *Journal of Bunka Gakuen University*.

Phillip Howerton is professor of English at Missouri State University-West Plains. His essays, reviews, and poems have appeared in numerous journals and books, such as *American History through Literature*, *Arkansas Review*, *Big Muddy*, *Christian Science Monitor*, *Encyclopedia of Arkansas History and Culture*, *Journal of Kentucky Studies*, *Midwest Quarterly*, *Red Rock Review*, *Slant*, and *Writers of the American Renaissance*. He is a co-founder and poetry editor of *Cave Region Review* and general editor of *Elder Mountain*. His poetry collection, *The History of Tree Roots*, was published by Golden Antelope Press in 2015, and his *The Literature of the Ozarks: An Anthology* was published by University of Arkansas Press in 2019, a project for which he received the Missouri Literary Award from the Missouri Library Association. He and his wife, Victoria, own and operate Cornerpost Press.

Mike Kaminski is a curious student of the Ozarks and a high school educator in Fayetteville, Arkansas. He enjoys hiking new trails and exploring Hamestring Creek with his wife and four children. He is a member of the Ozarks Writers League.

Rocky Macy grew up in the small tourist town of Noel in the Missouri Ozarks. He is a retired public-school educator, state child protection worker, and a licensed clinical civilian social worker with the U.S. military. Recently, *Crimes in Desolation*, a full-length historical drama that Macy wrote, was presented by the Spotlight Players at Seymour Johnson Air Force Base in Goldsboro, North Carolina. Macy is the father of three grown children and has six grandchildren. He lives in West Plains.

Lynn Morrow, M.A., Missouri State University, served as research historian for the Center for Ozarks Studies, managed the historic preservation consulting firm Kalen and Morrow, and administered Missouri's national model in public records preservation at the Missouri State Archives. Morrow has published widely in the *Missouri Historical Review*, *Gateway Heritage*, *Missouri Folklore Journal*, *Ozarks Watch*, *Big Muddy*, and in other serials, dictionaries, and anthologies. He co-edited two documentary histories, co-authored *Shepherd of the Hills Country: Tourism Transforms the Ozarks, 1880s-1930s* (University of Arkansas Press), and edited *The Ozarks in Missouri History: Discoveries in an American Region* (University of Missouri Press).

John Mort's first novel, *Soldier in Paradise* (1999), was widely reviewed and won the W. Y. Boyd Award for best military fiction. He has published seven other books, including two readers advisory works, two novels, and four collections of stories. His short stories have appeared in a wide variety of magazines, including *The New Yorker*, *Missouri Review*, the *Chicago Tribune*, the *Arkansas Review*, and in *Sixfold*. He is the winner of a National Endowment for the Arts literary grant, the Hackney Award, and a Western Writers of America Spur for the short story, "The Hog Whisperer." In 2017 he was awarded the Sullivan Prize for his short story collection, *Down Along the Piney*, which was published in 2018 by the University of Notre Dame Press. His novel *Oklahoma Odyssey* was released by University of Oklahoma Press in spring of 2022, and his *The Ballad of Johnny Bell* will be released by Cornerpost Press in October 2022. Mort served with the First Cavalry from 1968 through 1970 as a rifleman and RTO. He attended the University of Iowa, from which he earned a BA in English (1972), an MFA in writing (1974), and an MLS (1976). He worked as a librarian, editor, and teacher. He lives in Coweta, Oklahoma.

Tim Nutt is director of the Historical Research Center at the University of Arkansas for Medical Sciences. Previously, he was Head of Special Collections at the University of Arkansas-Fayetteville and founding Deputy Curator of the Butler Center for Arkansas Studies at the Central Arkansas Library System. He also served as the founding Managing Editor and Staff Historian of the award-winning online *Encyclopedia of Arkansas History & Culture*. A native of Bigelow, Arkansas, Nutt received a BA in history from the University of Central Arkansas and a master's in library science, with an emphasis on archives, from the University of Oklahoma. He is a past president of the Arkansas Historical Association and a certified archivist.

Gerry Sloan is a retired music professor living in Fayetteville, Arkansas. He has published five chapbooks (one translated into Mandarin) and two poetry collections: *Paper Lanterns* (2011) and *Crossings: A Memoir in Verse* (2017). His work has appeared in such literary magazines as *Arkansas Review, North Dakota Quarterly, The Kansas Quarterly, The Nebraska Review, Nebo, Slant,* and the *Anthology of Magazine Verse & Yearbook of American Poetry*. He received the WORDS Award for Poetry in 1990 from the Arkansas Literary Society. More recently his "Poem for Palestine" won first place in the Gaza Freedom Flotilla Literary Contest.

Terrell Tebbetts holds the Martha Heasley Cox Chair in American Literature at Lyon College. He has published over three dozen articles on American literature in several books and in journals such as *Philological Review, Southern Literary Journal, The F. Scott Fitzgerald Review, The Steinbeck Review,* and *The Faulkner Journal*. He regularly co-leads the Teaching Faulkner sessions at Ole Miss's annual Faulkner and Yoknapatawpha Conference.

Amy Wright Vollmar loves to search the nearby wild for poems (and interesting rocks) near Springfield, Missouri, where she lives with her family. She always carries a mud-proof notebook, and wears bug spray in lieu of perfume! Her poetry has previously appeared in *Elder Mountain* and the *Cave Region Review*, and her first book of poetry, *Follow*, was published by Cornerpost Press in 2020. Through her poems, she invites you to explore the fragile but tenacious wilderness of the Ozarks.

Drought 2022

Low Water Bridge

Spring Flood, Summer Drought

Tracks and Mudcracks

Swimming Hole